What's happening to Ashleigh?

"Why did you fall?" Cindy asked timidly.

Ashleigh sighed. "Oh, I just had a dizzy spell. I almost blacked out for a few seconds."

"Should we go to the hospital?" Mike asked quietly.

Ashleigh shook her head. "That's not necessary—I just need to rest. Let's go back to the bed-and-breakfast so I can lie down."

"You're lucky you fell off when you did," Mike said grimly.

"I suppose so." Ashleigh gave him a wry smile. "Glory got in at least part of a work."

"I meant you were so lucky that none of the horses trampled you," Mike said. "A group of two-year-olds was right behind you. Those horses are relatively inexperienced, and their jockeys barely stopped them from running over you."

"Yeah, that's true." Ashleigh's voice was subdued.

In the barn Ashleigh eased herself down on a bale of hay and turned to the group. "Maybe it's time I made an announcement," she said. . . .

Don't miss these exciting books from HarperPaperbacks!

Collect all the books in the THOROUGHBRED series:

#1 A Horse Called Wonder
#2 Wonder's Promise
#3 Wonder's First Race
#4 Wonder's Victory
#5 Ashleigh's Dream
#6 Wonder's Yearling
#7 Samantha's Pride
#8 Sierra's Steeplechase
#9 Pride's Challenge

#10 Pride's Last Race
#11 Wonder's Sister
#12 Shining's Orphan
#13 Cindy's Runaway Colt
#14 Cindy's Glory
#15 Glory's Triumph
#16 Glory in Danger
#17 Ashleigh's Farewell
#18 Glory's Rival*

THOROUGHBRED Super Editions:

Ashleigh's Christmas Miracle
Ashleigh's Diary
Ashleigh's Hope

Also by Joanna Campbell:

Battlecry Forever!
Star of Shadowbrook Farm

*coming soon

ATTENTION: ORGANIZATIONS AND CORPORATIONS

Most HarperPaperbacks are available at special quantity discounts for bulk purchases for sales promotions, premiums, or fund-raising. For information, please call or write:

**Special Markets Department, HarperCollins*Publishers*,
10 East 53rd Street, New York, N.Y. 10022
Telephone: (212) 207-7528. Fax: (212) 207-7222.**

THOROUGHBRED

ASHLEIGH'S FAREWELL

WRITTEN BY
KAREN BENTLEY

CREATED BY
JOANNA CAMPBELL

HarperPaperbacks
A Division of HarperCollins*Publishers*

HarperPaperbacks
A Division of HarperCollins*Publishers*
10 East 53rd Street, New York, N.Y. 10022-5299

This is a work of fiction. The characters, incidents, and dialogues are products of the author's imagination and are not to be construed as real. Any resemblance to actual events or persons, living or dead, is entirely coincidental.

ISBN 0-06-106397-5

HarperCollins®, ®, and HarperPaperbacks™ are trademarks of HarperCollins*Publishers* Inc.

Cover art: © 1996 Daniel Weiss Associates, Inc.

First HarperPaperbacks printing: October 1996

Printed in the United States of America

Visit HarperPaperbacks on the World Wide Web at
http://www.harpercollins.com/paperbacks

❖ 10 9 8 7 6 5 4 3 2 1

For John

"Ashleigh's so incredible!" twelve-year-old Cindy McLean said, leaning eagerly over the rail at the Saratoga racetrack. The summer meet would begin in a few days at the famous old New York track, and Ashleigh Griffen had just ridden March to Glory, the magnificent gray colt and Whitebrook Farm's newest superstar, out through the gap for his morning work. In the dim light just before dawn, Glory's sleek, dappled coat gleamed a subdued silver.

"Ashleigh's the best jockey in the business," agreed Samantha McLean, Cindy's eighteen-year-old sister. Her green eyes sparkled with pleasure.

"Glory's raring to go." Cindy picked up her binoculars so that she could see the colt better as he and Ashleigh rounded the clubhouse turn. The powerful young horse was tugging impatiently at the reins, trying to break from the slow warm-up trot into a gallop. "Take it easy, Glory!" Cindy called. With a toss of his head, Glory seemed to ignore her words.

But Ashleigh expertly held the colt back and turned him to the outside of the track, where other horses were warming up. Glory had gotten his own way for no more than a stride, Cindy noted.

"Think Glory will put in the fastest work today?" Ian McLean asked as he joined Cindy and Samantha at the rail. Both girls turned to smile at their father. Ian, together with Mike Reese, Ashleigh's husband, and Ashleigh, had made Whitebrook one of the most successful breeding and training farms in Kentucky.

"I know he'll be the fastest!" Cindy declared. She shivered with excitement even though the July air was thick with warmth and humidity. Glory, she was sure, not only would put in a black-type work—the fastest work of the day at the track—but would win his next race, the Jim Dandy, scheduled in less than two weeks.

Cindy was thrilled that Glory would be racing in a major stakes race at the Saratoga track, renowned for races that had been run for a century or more. If the colt came out of that race well, he'd run in another race there, then go on to even bigger races at Belmont. In the beginning of November he'd race in the Breeders' Cup Classic, the richest race of the year.

As she adjusted her binoculars to watch Ashleigh gallop Glory along the backside, Cindy smiled to herself. Glory had come a long way since the past winter, when he was an untried colt at the Keeneland auction with an uncertain fate. In those days Cindy had been the only one who had any confidence in Glory as a racehorse.

The colt picked up speed as he rounded the far turn. "What's Glory doing today?" Cindy asked.

"Ashleigh's going to work him three-eighths of a mile," Mike said, coming over from the gap to the track, where he had been instructing another exercise rider. Ashleigh's blond husband wore an excited smile on his face. "Ashleigh should be letting him out in a second. They're coming up on the three-eighths pole . . . there they go!"

Cindy tensed with anticipation. Nothing was more beautiful to her than seeing Glory run.

The big gray colt shot past the three-eighths pole just as the sun lifted above the horizon, flooding the track with brilliant yellow light. Glory's strides lengthened as Ashleigh expertly cued him, letting out just enough rein and positioning her body over his withers.

Glory looked like a silver express train as he flashed around the turn, Cindy thought, gripping the rail tightly. As Glory's exercise rider back home, she remembered so well how it felt to be on the powerful colt as his graceful strides ate up the ground. Glory pounded into the stretch.

"He couldn't be going better," Mike commented.

Cindy opened her mouth to agree—and gasped in horror. Ashleigh was reeling in the saddle! Cindy saw Ashleigh grip Glory's mane, fighting to keep her balance.

For an instant Cindy thought Ashleigh would regain control. Then she slumped forward and fell, hitting the ground with a sickening impact. Glory leaped sideways in fright, then galloped on, reins dangling.

Ashleigh tried to rise, but crumpled to the ground. "Ashleigh!" Cindy screamed. Glory had never once thrown Ashleigh, and certainly not during an ordinary work!

Glory flew by the gap, riderless. Cindy stared at him in disbelief. She still couldn't take in what had happened.

"Cindy, get the horse!" Mike cried, already running out onto the track. "I'll help Ashleigh."

Cindy's heart was pounding with fear for Ashleigh, but she knew that Glory had to be caught quickly. He was still running at full speed down the crowded track. If he hit another horse or rider, it could mean disaster for everyone involved.

Cindy looked quickly to her left before she crossed the track. Three riders who hadn't seen the accident were barreling around the far turn, headed straight for Ashleigh.

I don't have time to warn them, Cindy thought desperately. *And if I run out there, I might cause another accident!*

At the last second the riders saw the fallen jockey. They swerved their horses, barely missing her.

"Oh, thank goodness!" Cindy cried. Now if she could only get Glory before something happened to him. Cindy glanced both ways again and ran along the track, her boots sinking in the soft dirt. She stayed near the outside rail, where the horses were moving the slowest.

Glory had galloped about a quarter mile up the track. That was where Ashleigh usually turned him after a work. Glory was carrying his head and tail high and snorting nervously. He was obviously rattled by his jockey's fall.

With a sigh of relief Cindy saw that Glory was going to turn himself that morning. The colt began making a loop at an easy gallop. "Glory!" she called. "Over here, boy!"

Glory craned his neck around and whinnied. By now all the riders on the track knew that a horse was loose, and they had slowed their mounts to a walk to make Cindy's task easier. Glory trotted over to Cindy, stirrups flapping.

"Good boy." Cindy grabbed the colt's reins and turned him toward the gap. Ashleigh was sitting up, supported by Mike and Samantha. *She's not badly hurt!* Cindy thought.

Cindy quickly looked Glory over. The colt was moving easily on his slender, powerful legs and blowing lightly. He hadn't even broken into a sweat—he seemed fine after his riderless work. Cindy had thought he would be. Glory had actually done less running than they'd planned for him that morning, and with less weight on his back.

"Are you all right?" Cindy called anxiously to Ashleigh as they approached. Mike and Samantha were helping Ashleigh off the track.

"I think so." Ashleigh managed a wobbly smile. "Just shaken up. Is Glory okay?"

"He's fine." Cindy lovingly brushed back Glory's

thick black-and-gray mane and stroked his smooth, dappled neck. The colt lowered his head and lipped her other hand, probably looking for the treat she gave him after every work. As far as Glory was concerned, this day was almost like every other. "I'd better cool him out," Cindy said.

Ashleigh nodded. "We'll come with you."

Glory's shod hooves clopped quietly on the dew-drenched ground as the group walked slowly to the backside. Glory pushed Cindy affectionately with his nose. He seemed to have gotten over his scare at Ashleigh's fall.

But what about Ashleigh? Cindy worried. Ashleigh was still extremely pale. "Why did you fall?" Cindy asked timidly. She didn't want to sound critical.

Ashleigh sighed. "Oh, I just had a dizzy spell. I almost blacked out for a few seconds."

"Should we go to the hospital?" Mike asked quietly.

Ashleigh shook her head. "That's not necessary—I just need to rest. Let's go back to the bed-and-breakfast so I can lie down."

"You're lucky you fell off when you did," Mike said grimly.

"I suppose so." Ashleigh gave him a wry smile. "Glory got in at least part of a work."

"I meant you were lucky that none of the horses trampled you," Mike said. "A group of two-year-olds was right behind you. Those horses are relatively inexperienced, and their jockeys barely stopped them from running over you."

Cindy glanced quickly at Ashleigh. Cindy didn't

understand why Mike would bring up something that Ashleigh must know.

"Yeah, that's true." Ashleigh's voice was subdued.

"Well, no harm done," Samantha said sympathetically, tightening her grip on Ashleigh's arm.

In the barn Ashleigh eased herself down on a bale of hay and turned to the group. "Maybe it's time I made an announcement," she said.

"I'll cool out Glory if you want," Len, the stable manager, said to Cindy as he walked out of the feed room.

"This will only take a few seconds, and Glory's not very hot," Ashleigh said. "Besides, I'd like Len—and maybe Glory—to hear this, too."

The stable manager sat beside Ashleigh on the hay bale and gave her a warm smile. "Want to give me three guesses about what you're going to say?" he asked.

"No." Ashleigh laughed. "I'll bet you could guess with one. I don't want you to steal my thunder."

Cindy frowned. Maybe Len knew what Ashleigh was going to say, but Cindy couldn't imagine. She knew it must have something to do with why Ashleigh had just fallen. That couldn't be good. But Ashleigh looked happy.

Ashleigh massaged her temples, then looked up. "I have some big news for everybody. Well, almost everybody—Mike knows."

"Knows what?" Samantha asked eagerly.

"We're expecting a baby in January." Ashleigh looked at Mike and smiled. "I just found out for sure."

Cindy stared at Ashleigh in amazement. A baby! That was great news. But it was so soon. When would Ashleigh be able to ride again?

"I wanted to ride Glory in just one more race, even though it would have been a risk," Ashleigh continued. "He doesn't go well for anybody else, and I would have had to back out on such short notice. But I guess I was pushing it by riding."

"You were," Mike confirmed, putting his arm around her shoulders.

Cindy quickly calculated in her head. Ashleigh wouldn't be able to ride until at least January—no, longer, because she would have to recover after she had the baby. That was all the way through the racing season. Ashleigh might not be able to ride for a year!

Cindy pressed her cheek to Glory's soft black muzzle, trying to still the worry rising within her. She'd had such wonderful visions of Glory's next victories at Saratoga and at Belmont, and of his crowning triumph in November at the Breeders' Cup. But now Ashleigh wouldn't be riding in any of those races.

"What are we going to do, boy?" Cindy murmured as everyone crowded around Ashleigh to congratulate her. "Will you run your fastest for someone else?"

The next morning Cindy brushed and tacked up Glory for his exercise ride. Mike and Ian wanted to work the colt again, since Ashleigh's accident the day before had cut short his exercise.

"Somebody new is going to ride you," Cindy told Glory. "I want you to be on your best behavior."

Glory eyed her and gently leaned into the crossties, trying to get closer to her. He seemed to be in a calm mood, Cindy thought. Probably that was because he'd gotten a fairly good run in the previous day.

She stepped outside the barn to check the weather. A heavy mist had hidden the track when she'd arrived an hour before to do chores, and she had no idea what to expect.

The blinding circle of the sun was coming up, shooting out yellow and white banners. The horses already on the track were silhouettes edged in gold, shimmering in the dissipating fog.

Ashleigh was just approaching the shed row. Cindy walked over to join her.

"It's superb, isn't it?" Ashleigh was watching the sunrise, too.

"It sure is." Cindy looked at Ashleigh a little shyly. She wasn't quite sure how to treat Ashleigh now that she was pregnant.

Glory pranced across the stable yard with a young, dark-haired woman up. "Who's riding Glory?" Cindy asked Ashleigh.

"That's Kelly Morgan. We're going to try her as Glory's new jockey," Ashleigh said.

Cindy bit her lip.

"Don't look so worried, Cindy." Ashleigh smiled reassuringly. "I'll still be here to help out. I'm not going to disappear."

9

Cindy smiled back uncertainly and glanced over at Glory. The new jockey hadn't taken him to the track yet. Either she was waiting to talk to Ashleigh or Glory wouldn't let her take him out. Cindy could see that the colt was full of himself that morning. He was arching his neck, trying to get more rein, and hopping on his front feet as the jockey attempted to circle him.

Glory looked beautiful and spirited when he acted up, but Cindy frowned with concern. Soon Glory would be facing the biggest races of his career—of any horse's career. His next race, the Jim Dandy, was a grade-one race against a highly competitive field. A day earlier Cindy wouldn't have worried about Glory's chances. He'd won his last race brilliantly at Belmont in June, coming from behind after a bad stumble at the gate to score a victory by several lengths.

But that had been with Ashleigh riding. Cindy felt a rush of alarm now as Glory almost bumped another horse and exercise rider on the busy backside.

"Watch out!" The other rider yanked hard on his horse, barely avoiding Glory's flank.

Cindy almost cried out. Now she was really worried that Glory was dangerously out of control. If the two horses had collided, Glory might have kicked out, injuring both of them.

Glory's never been easy to ride, Cindy thought as she watched the new jockey tugging on Glory's reins, trying to get him in hand. *But that's because his life has been so hard.*

Before Cindy had known Glory, he had been stolen from his original owners and badly abused in training. Glory had finally broken away from the thieves, and Cindy had found him wandering in the woods near Whitebrook.

She had secretly trained the colt, hiding him in a shed at Whitebrook. It had taken Cindy months to restore the colt's trust in people again, and he was still wary of strangers. But after Glory showed amazing speed on the Whitebrook track, the farm had bought him at the Keeneland auction the previous January.

Cindy had thought her problems with Glory were over until Glory's official training had begun. The colt still seemed to have bad memories of the track and was so insecure he bolted from every shadow. With guidance from Glory's first trainer, Ben Cavell, Ashleigh and Cindy had gotten Glory over his fears. Glory had won his first race by twenty lengths and set a stakes record.

Cindy had thought nothing could stop Glory then, but just a month before, the colt had tested positive for drugs at the Belmont track. Ian McLean, as Glory's official trainer, had been held responsible for the drugging and had been suspended from training. Finally Cindy and her sixth-grade classmate, Max Smith, had solved the mystery of who was drugging Glory. Cindy and Max had caught the culprit trying to kill Glory with a drug and had come close to being killed themselves.

Cindy had hoped Glory was past all that trouble.

But watching the colt fuss and fight his rider now, she felt the old uncertainty about his chances.

"Is Glory ready to go?" Mike asked as he walked up to Cindy and Ashleigh.

"I think so—let me just talk to Kelly a minute." Ashleigh nodded in the direction of Glory's new jockey. "Come on over, Kelly!" Ashleigh called.

Kelly rode Glory over to the group. She wasn't letting Glory run away with her, Cindy noted, but the colt still wasn't settling down. He was trotting in slow motion, high-stepping, and flicking his tail nervously.

As Glory approached, he suddenly saw Cindy. With a snort and a toss of his head, the big colt walked eagerly forward, his gait finally smooth and relaxed. He stopped abruptly in front of Cindy and nudged her.

"Yes, I'm glad to see you, too," Cindy said, rubbing Glory's velvety black muzzle. "But you've got to behave yourself, boy—you've got a job to do on the track now."

The big horse nodded as if he understood, then half closed his dark eyes, leaning into her caresses. Cindy ran her hands over Glory's glossy neck, savoring the softness of his healthy, silky coat.

"I think I know who you are," Kelly said, laughing. "Cindy McLean—Glory's groom, exercise rider, and favorite person."

"I told Kelly that if I can't ride Glory, I think she's the next-best choice," Ashleigh said.

Cindy nodded. She hoped so.

"Let's get on with Glory's gallop." Ian walked

over to the group. "If we can tear him away from Cindy, that is."

Cindy grinned. She loved the special bond she had with her horse. "Okay, Glory," she said, giving the colt a final pat and a little push on the shoulder. "Go out there and show everyone what you can do."

The colt huffed out a quick snort, as if he were miffed at being ordered away. Then he turned and marched in the direction of the track. With Glory's long stride, he passed most of the other horses heading out. Kelly pointed him through the gap.

Kelly seems okay, Cindy thought as she walked to the track with Ian, Ashleigh, and Mike. *Maybe this will work out fine.*

As if Ashleigh were reading her mind, Ashleigh said, "Kelly has an excellent record as a jockey. She's ridden mostly on the West Coast, at Santa Anita, Del Mar, and Hollywood Park. Last month she notched a grade-one victory in the California Stakes at Hollywood Park."

"Wow!" Cindy knew that the California Stakes was a prestigious race with a rich purse.

"There's no substitute for Ashleigh, but Kelly will have to do in the meantime," Mike said, squeezing Ashleigh's arm.

"Congratulations, Mike," Cindy said shyly. In the confusion after Ashleigh's announcement the day before, she'd forgotten to congratulate him as well as Ashleigh.

"Thanks." Mike smiled broadly. "We're looking forward to being a family of three."

13

When they reached the track, Cindy leaned on the rail, studying Glory intently. Kelly was trotting the colt counterclockwise to the outside. She was patting Glory's neck and talking to him. Cindy noticed that Glory seemed relaxed and was responding to Kelly's commands.

"He's looking good," Samantha commented, joining Cindy at the rail.

Cindy smiled at her sister. "Yeah, he seems to be enjoying himself." She watched Glory float by, a sleek gray silhouette in the misty morning. He was still moving at an easy, ground-eating trot. Cindy pulled her blond hair back into a ponytail and relaxed. She turned her face for a moment to the sun, which was rising through a filter of gauzy pink clouds.

When she opened her eyes again, Glory's quick, long strides had already put him and Kelly on the far side of the track. Kelly increased their pace to a slow gallop.

Cindy leaned forward to look at Ian. "Dad, what's Glory going to do today?"

"Just a short session—I don't want to push him too hard, especially since he had part of a work yesterday. We'll have him do an easy gallop for three furlongs." Ian picked up his binoculars. "On the other hand, we've got to keep him sharp. I'd like very much to see Glory run in the Breeders' Cup. And to do that, he has to win several races in a short time. The Breeders' Cup is in just three and a half months."

"Glory's lagging in the points standings for the

14

Breeders' Cup," Mike commented. "A lot of horses entered in the Classic are ahead of him."

Cindy knew that the top eight horses in the points standings would run in the Breeders' Cup Classic, which was a mile and a quarter. Ten points were awarded for first place in grade-one races, six points for second, and four points for third. Glory had to win a lot more points to be in the top eight. Six other horses would be selected by committee to run in the Classic, but it was a much surer bet to have accumulated a lot of points.

"We'll have to hope for luck," Mike continued. "For Glory to make the cutoff for the Breeders' Cup, some of the horses who are beating him in points have to lose while he wins."

"It's chancy," Ian acknowledged.

Glory and Kelly were approaching the quarter-mile pole. The colt pricked up his ears. "He knows what's coming," Cindy murmured.

The instant Glory passed the marker, he sprang into an energetic gallop.

"Attaboy!" Cindy said proudly.

"So far, so good," Samantha agreed.

Glory picked up the pace. His long mane and tail streamed behind him as he changed leads and pounded down the stretch.

Cindy leaned around Samantha again. "I thought you said he was just supposed to do an easy gallop," she said to her dad.

"Those were Kelly's instructions," Ian confirmed with a frown.

"Glory's doing better than a twelve clip," Mike said tensely. "Damn! Slow him down!"

Cindy gripped the rail, willing Glory to slow down. A twelve clip, she knew, was when a horse ran several furlongs, each in twelve seconds. The longer the horse kept it up, the more difficult and strenuous it was. The famous racehorse Northern Dancer had won the Kentucky Derby in two minutes, a twelve-clip over a mile and a quarter. That was considered tremendously fast.

Suddenly Glory dropped back into a slow gallop. Just ahead of him Cindy saw a group of horses leaving the track. Glory had obviously seen them, too, and headed right for them. Kelly barely managed to steer the gamboling colt around them.

"What was that?" Mike asked, sounding bewildered when Kelly rode up to them.

"I'm sorry. I didn't want to hold him so hard he got frustrated," Kelly explained.

As Cindy gathered Glory's reins to take him to the backside, she thought the colt looked pleased with himself. *No wonder. You had a nice little run, then you visited with some other horses.* Cindy frowned. That wasn't the way the gallop was supposed to have gone at all.

Mike ran his hands over Glory's legs. "We'll see how he comes out of this," he said.

"Ashleigh filled me in on his history. I thought he needed a gentle hand," Kelly said defensively.

Cindy groaned silently. Glory *did* need a gentle hand—but he also needed a very firm one. Glory had

16

seen that he could take full advantage of Kelly. The next time he might be even worse.

"Well, let's try again in a couple of days," Ian said with a sigh.

Kelly nodded. "I've got to find my next mount. I'll stop by the barn later if you want to discuss this further."

"Please do," Mike said.

"I'll talk to Kelly about her riding style," Ashleigh said when the jockey had walked back over to the gap. "I'm sure she can make some adjustments and put in a good ride."

But Cindy noticed Ashleigh's worried frown. *I wonder if Ashleigh really believes that, considering the way Glory just acted,* Cindy thought. *This isn't a good beginning at all.*

2

"Cindy, you've been sitting around for hours. What are you planning to do today?" Beth McLean asked Cindy a few days after Kelly's first track disaster with Glory.

Cindy looked up from her comfortable wicker chair at the bed-and-breakfast. The McLeans had been staying at the warm, homey B&B since they arrived at Saratoga three weeks earlier. Cindy liked sitting in the living room, with its cheerful red-and-white curtains and bright geraniums on the windowsills. She'd sat there most of the afternoon, staring out the window at the luxuriant old trees in the yard and wondering what to do about Glory.

Kelly's first bad ride on the colt hadn't been the last. Glory had put in a bad work for Kelly just the day before, again going much faster than Mike and Ian wanted. After the strenuous work Glory had had a little heat in his right foreleg. If Glory continued to

18

stress the leg, he might be out for his next race or even the season.

"I guess we'll have to find another jockey," Ashleigh had said unhappily as Len coaxed Glory into accepting an ice boot around his injured leg. "I hate to do that—I think Glory responds to consistency—but this obviously isn't working out."

That morning Cindy had walked Glory around the barns, talking to him and wishing he would shape up. Her words wouldn't do much good, she knew. At least the heat was completely gone from Glory's leg—for now. There was no telling what would happen when they worked him again.

Cindy looked at Beth now and shrugged. "I don't have any special plans today. I'll go back to the track later this afternoon and help Len with the chores."

"Why don't you do something before then?" Beth suggested. "How about taking a walk?"

"I don't want to—it looks like rain." Cindy picked up a fashion magazine from the end table and leafed through it. She knew she wasn't scoring points with Beth by sitting around. Beth was an aerobics instructor in Lexington and an active person.

Beth looked exasperated. She sighed. "Cindy, it isn't like you to be so down in the dumps. Try not to worry so much about Glory," she said gently. "He's a very talented horse, and your dad, Mike, and Ashleigh are the best trainers in the business. They'll figure out what to do."

Cindy let the magazine drop. Beth was right, she realized. "In a couple of days Ashleigh's going to try another jockey—Albert Henderson," she said, hope creeping into her voice. "Maybe Glory will stop playing around for him."

"You see?" Beth nodded. "I think he will. Oh, I forgot! A letter came for you this morning." Beth picked up an envelope from the end table next to Cindy.

Cindy took the letter, recognizing right away Max's careful handwriting. She was glad to hear from her friend. Max and his mother, who was Whitebrook's vet, had been at the summer Belmont meet but had returned to Kentucky several weeks earlier. Cindy had sent Max a postcard since then but hadn't heard back.

She quickly tore open the letter.

July 23
Dear Cindy,
How have you been? What's new at Saratoga? Hey, did you hear that the two guys who tried to kill Glory got jail sentences? So I guess they won't be bothering him for a while.

Cindy frowned. That was good news, but the trainer who had masterminded the plot, Joe Gallagher, had gotten off scot-free. No one had been able to prove anything against him. The trainer had wanted Glory out of the way so that his best horse, Flightful, could win more races. Cindy remembered with a shiver that Joe would almost certainly be back from the West Coast, where Flightful was currently running, for the Breeders' Cup in November.

But she knew that Mike, Ashleigh, and Ian would have tight security around Glory's stall then. That problem seemed under control. Cindy turned back to the letter.

I've been going on rounds a lot with my mom. She said she'll be glad when you get back to help, too. (Watch out!)

Cindy glanced up from her reading at a noise on the stairs. The Whitebrook group occupied three of the suites at the B&B, two downstairs and one on the second floor. The second upstairs suite had been rented the day before by a pleasant-looking couple in their thirties.

They waved hello, and Cindy smiled back. She remembered that Ian had said the couple were trainers based at Del Mar in California.

Cindy saw to her surprise that a dark-haired girl about her own age was with them. She must have missed seeing her the previous day when the couple checked in. The girl wore a black jean miniskirt with black tights, a gold-spangled T-shirt from the Del Mar track, and chunky black sandals. She looked very sophisticated.

Suddenly Cindy was aware of her worn jeans, dirty from the morning's chores, her beat-up sneakers, and her Churchill Downs T-shirt, washed until it had faded to a pale green because she loved to wear it.

Cindy smiled uncertainly at the girl. The girl looked right through her, then said something to her parents. A moment later the door banged shut behind them.

How stuck-up can you get? Cindy thought. She shrugged and returned to her letter.

Tell me when you're coming back to Whitebrook to get Sierra. Maybe we can go for a ride.
Your friend,
Max

Cindy looked at the letter for another moment. In a little over a week, the day after the Jim Dandy, she would drive back to Kentucky with Samantha and Mike to get Sierra for the New York Turf Writers Steeplechase at Saratoga. Then she could ride with Max or the horses at Whitebrook. Cindy felt a quick flutter of anticipation at the thought of riding again. It seemed like ages since she'd been on a horse—since the beginning of summer.

"If only I could ride Glory," Cindy murmured. She was sure the colt would go well under his familiar rider. But Cindy couldn't ride at the track until she was sixteen.

She thought of Ben Cavell, Glory's first trainer. He'd been able to help her with Glory before. Ben was running his horses out at Del Mar, but Cindy had gotten his home address when she'd stayed at his farm earlier in the summer. *Maybe if I sent a letter to the farm, it would be forwarded to the California track,* she said to herself. If not, she would just have to wait to ask his advice until Ben came to Saratoga. He had mentioned that he'd be bringing his horses there sometime during the meet.

But by then Glory will probably have run his next race, Cindy thought. She uncapped a pen and shook her head. She just had to hope her letter reached Ben in time.

"Glory, hold still," Cindy pleaded, tightening her grip on the reins. It was three days later, and Ian, Mike, and Ashleigh planned to work Glory with the new jockey, Albert Henderson. Working the colt so soon after the injury to his foreleg was risky, but the race was less than a week away. Mike, Ian, and Ashleigh had to give Albert at least one trial run.

Glory skittered sideways, flaring his nostrils. The colt definitely didn't like the looks of the seasoned jockey. When Albert had first walked up to Glory in the barn, the colt had tried to take a bite out of him. Glory hadn't bitten anybody in months, Cindy thought. She chewed a fingernail with worry.

Now Glory wouldn't let Albert get on. The colt backed up and nervously pawed the ground.

"Box him in," Mike directed. Cindy held Glory's head while Mike and Ian stood at Glory's flanks. Albert leaped nimbly into the saddle and gathered the reins.

Cindy could see that Glory wasn't happy about it. He bowed his neck and began backing again. Albert gave Glory a swift, hard kick, and the colt jumped forward.

Cindy swallowed hard. Albert had barely begun to

ride, but she already doubted he would work out as Glory's jockey.

Albert forced Glory to walk to the track. A light sweat had broken out on the colt's neck. He fought Albert at almost every stride, twisting his neck and hauling on the reins.

Cindy watched in horror as Glory and his new jockey lurched around the track in a contest of wills. Glory constantly threw up his head, but Albert yanked it down every time with the reins.

Eyes rolling with fright, Glory thundered down the track. Albert still had the colt under an iron hold. Glory was twisting his head wildly from side to side, trying to free himself from the restraint.

I sure didn't need to worry about Glory playing around the way he did with Kelly, Cindy thought. *He's too terrified to have any fun!*

"Let the horse out a little!" Mike yelled. He ran a hand through his thick blond hair in frustration.

"I can't believe what you let him get away with out there."

Cindy turned quickly at the sound of the familiar, scornful voice. Brad Townsend stood next to her, watching Glory closely. For years Brad, the son of Townsend Acres owner Clay Townsend, had been in disputes with Whitebrook, particularly Ashleigh. When Ashleigh was Cindy's age, her parents had been breeding managers at Townsend Acres, a wealthy, huge breeding and training farm near Lexington. Ashleigh had made Ashleigh's Wonder, the foal everyone else had thought would die or be worthless, into a champion racehorse. After Wonder won the Breeders' Cup Classic, Clay Townsend had given Ashleigh a half interest in Wonder.

Soon after the deal was made, the problems between Ashleigh and Brad had begun. They had never agreed on how Wonder, and then her offspring Townsend Pride, Townsend Princess, and Mr. Wonderful, should be trained. Wonder now had a new, gorgeous colt, Wonder's Champion, who at just two months old already showed great promise. Right after he was born, Ashleigh had said the battle was already heating up about where he would be trained—at Whitebrook or Townsend Acres. Since each farm owned half of him, it was hard to say where he would go.

Brad wore jeans and a helmet and was holding one of Townsend Acres' horses, Dandy as He Does, a well-made bay stakes runner. Cindy had to admit that Brad was an excellent rider and a hands-on manager at their farm. He trained and worked the horses himself instead of leaving those jobs to stable hands.

Cindy looked back out at the track and almost cried out. Glory was bolting down the stretch for the wire, still shaking his head furiously. He was obviously in pain.

"Why has Albert got him up so tight?" Mike asked in disbelief.

"Because the horse is running away," Brad said. Cindy noticed that he kept his voice down so that Mike didn't hear. She knew there was no love lost between Brad and Mike because of the way Brad treated Ashleigh.

Go away! Cindy willed Brad. Why would he want to watch such a terrible work anyway, except to make jabs about Whitebrook's horses and training? But Brad stayed put, saying nothing, his eyes fixed on Glory.

Cindy began to feel uneasy. Brad had never once said anything positive about Glory, but he had shown up at several of Glory's works. Ben Cavell had told Cindy that Brad knew a good horse when he saw one, so that might be the reason, she guessed. That seemed unlike Brad, though. He had nothing to gain by watching Glory.

"Okay, Albert—bring him back!" Mike yelled as Glory whipped past the wire.

Ian glanced at his stopwatch.

"What was Glory's time?" Cindy asked. She was sure it had been fast, despite the problems with the ride.

"Just over twenty-three for the quarter mile—very decent," Mike said, shrugging.

"It doesn't really matter." Ian looked discouraged. "If Glory acts like that in a race, he'll use himself up. He has to go nine furlongs in his next race, not two."

Albert was bringing Glory back over to the gap. The colt was still full of fight, Cindy noted with dismay. Glory's eyes glittered. He continued to yank on the reins.

Cindy hurried to meet him. The big horse's neck was lathered with sweat, and his nostrils showed red as he heaved out breaths. *He's a wreck,* Cindy realized

26

with a sinking heart. Her dad was definitely right—the colt would never make it through a whole race like that.

"Steady, boy," she said soothingly, taking the reins as Albert dismounted. "You're okay."

Brad led his horse in the direction of the backside, shaking his head. Ian and Mike ignored him while they talked with Albert. The jockey gestured hopelessly with his hands, then walked off.

"I think we're going to have to ask Kelly to ride Glory again," Ian said wearily. "Glory didn't go well for her, but I don't know another jockey who could handle him better at this point."

"We don't have time for Kelly to give Glory another work before he races," Mike said. His brow was furrowed with concern.

"You mean . . ." Cindy hesitated. She couldn't think how to say it. Kelly couldn't handle Glory even in a work, but she was going to ride him in a race?

"I don't think we have any choice about using Kelly," Ian said. "We've talked to her about taking a firmer hand with Glory, and he may go better for her in the race." He didn't look very optimistic.

Gently Cindy rubbed Glory's shoulder. The colt was still trembling with nervous energy. "I'll cool him out," she said.

"Thanks, sweetie." Ian nodded. "He sure needs it."

Cindy examined Glory closely as they walked back to the shed row. The colt was slowly settling down as they got away from the track. His steps were relaxing, and his eyes were gentle again.

"Glory, what are we going to do? That was a terrible work—even worse than you did for Kelly," Cindy scolded. Every rider who got on Glory was just making the colt more determined to have his way, she realized.

Glory blew into her hair affectionately. *At least he still trusts me,* Cindy thought.

She walked Glory around and around the barns to cool him out. That day it took an hour—twice the time he usually needed, because he had been so upset. The longer the problems with jockeys went on, the longer it took to get him back to himself, Cindy decided. She had to do something to break the vicious cycle.

Cindy's eyes lit up. "I know what might work," she said.

She gave Glory a good brushing and put him in his stall. The colt gave a little sigh of contentment and began nibbling the last few strands of hay in his net.

Cindy hesitated a moment, looking up and down the stable aisle. No one was around. Len had gone to deal with the delivery of a grain shipment, since Cindy was there to keep an eye on the horses.

She looked back at Glory. "Move over near the wall, boy," she requested, gently pushing on his right flank. "I want to try something."

Glory obligingly shifted to about a foot from the wall. Cindy squeezed by him, then pushed her foot against the boards. Gripping Glory's mane, she pulled herself onto his back.

Glory twisted his head around to look at her.

"Do you remember what it's like to want a rider on your back?" Cindy asked.

28

The big gray horse bobbed his head, as if to say, *Now I do.*

Carefully Cindy cued Glory to walk around the stall, pressing with her inside leg so that he kept to the outside. Glory moved as calmly as if he were a pony giving rides at an amusement park.

"Why aren't you like this on the track?" Cindy asked with a sigh. But of course she knew why—because neither she nor Ashleigh, the two people Glory trusted and responded to, was riding him.

After a couple of circuits Cindy slid to the ground. At least she felt reassured about one thing—Glory was still himself. He could still get out on the track and run like the wind if they could just find the right rider for him.

Cindy opened the stall door and looked down the aisle. Two stalls down, Shining's exquisite head was poking over her half-door.

"Hey, girl," Cindy said, walking over to caress the roan mare. She had always loved Shining, the first Thoroughbred she'd ridden and groomed. Shining was such a beautiful color, Cindy thought. The mare's red and white flecked coat blended into her black legs, and she had a long, luxuriant black mane and tail. Shining was a half-sister to Wonder and Samantha's champion racehorse.

"I know you're ready for the Whitney," Cindy said. Shining had won the Suburban at Belmont in early July and was scheduled to run in the Whitney, her next big race, in ten days.

Cindy knew that the farm's financial troubles were

over now that Shining was racing in stakes again. She could see in her father's and Mike's expressions that a big load had been taken off everyone's mind.

Cindy glanced down the shed row. "Where's Matchless?" she wondered aloud. Like Shining and Glory, the chestnut colt usually looked out of his stall the moment he heard her voice, hoping for petting or treats. Moving down the aisle, she saw that Matchless was standing in his stall with his tail to her.

"What's the matter, handsome guy?" Cindy asked, slipping inside the stall. "I know Shining and Glory get most of the attention, but you're a star, too." Matchless had won an allowance race at Belmont and would run soon in a grade-two stakes at Saratoga.

Cindy rubbed the colt's ears just in front of his bridle path, the way he liked it. "That's better, right?" she asked as she closed the stall door behind her. Matchless turned around to watch her go.

Whitebrook has a lot of great horses, Cindy thought as she walked back to Glory's stall. She began to feel better about Glory. After all, he had run brilliantly in his last race. The problem of finding the right jockey for him was just a temporary setback.

"Hi there."

Cindy looked up to see Ashleigh. "Hi," she said. "How are you feeling?"

Ashleigh laughed. "Not you, too! Mike asks me that about every other minute. I feel pretty much the same as always, thank you. And I'm not made of glass."

"That's good." Cindy wondered if Ashleigh

missed riding. Maybe not too much, she thought. Having a baby was so exciting.

"I do have some news." Ashleigh frowned. "I'm going back to Whitebrook for several weeks. I'll leave tomorrow."

Cindy gasped. That couldn't be true. "But then you'll miss Glory's race!" Glory needed Ashleigh more than ever in his training.

"I don't want to go, with Glory's situation the way it is," Ashleigh said. Her voice was strained. "But I have to. The Townsends are causing trouble about Wonder's Champion."

"What kind of trouble?" Cindy asked, although she thought she could guess.

"It's the old argument with them about where Wonder's offspring will stay—at Whitebrook or Townsend Acres," Ashleigh said with a heavy sigh.

Cindy knew that Ashleigh wanted fiercely to keep the gorgeous colt at Whitebrook, especially since Mr. Wonderful, Wonder's only sound offspring, still hadn't come back to form for his two-year-old season after straining a tendon that spring.

"You deserve to keep Wonder's Champion after all the mistakes the Townsends made with Wonder and her other foals," Cindy said quickly.

"I know. I'm not about to forget the way Brad had Wonder whipped until she wouldn't run at all, or how Mr. Townsend nearly ruined Pride overracing him." Ashleigh was silent for a moment.

Cindy thought Ashleigh probably didn't even want to talk about the worst disaster of all with

Wonder's offspring—what had happened to Townsend Princess. Lavinia Townsend, Brad's headstrong wife and an unskilled rider, had taken the green filly out to exercise her. The young horse had gotten out of control and broken her leg. Princess's leg had then tragically been rebroken in a race in the spring. Princess was mending, but her health was still fragile. She would never run again.

"The Townsends should understand why you want to keep Wonder's Champion with you," Cindy said, biting a fingernail. She knew Ashleigh had to go back to Kentucky or the Townsends would probably get their way with the new colt. But of Glory's trainers, Ashleigh knew the colt best. Now there would really be no one to mediate between Glory's personality and the different riders Ian and Mike tried on him.

"The Townsends don't understand at all why Wonder's foals should stay with me," Ashleigh said. "I've had to fight for every one. And as half owners of any foal of Wonder's, they have as much right as I do to keep the colt." Ashleigh shrugged. "Let's not worry about it right now. I'll go back to Kentucky and scope out the Townsends' position. Maybe I can think of something to offer them in exchange for having Wonder's Champion stay at Whitebrook."

Cindy wondered what that could be. She was sure Wonder's Champion was a colt beyond price.

3

The next day Cindy stood on the wood porch of the bed-and-breakfast, looking out at the damp, gray weather. She stretched out her hands under the porch roof to gather the fine, blowing mist. Cindy had seen on the weather report the night before that thunder-showers were predicted for the following day, when the Jim Dandy would be run. Mike and Ian weren't any closer to finding a solution to Glory's jockey problem, and Ashleigh had left for Kentucky.

That morning hadn't been a good omen that the problem with Glory would right itself. Cindy had only walked the colt, but he had skittered and bounced on the lead line, thoroughly testing her. She'd really had to work to get him to settle down.

Beth opened the door and looked out. "Cindy! Brunch!"

"I'm coming." Cindy slid her hand along the wet wood rail, sending a shower of droplets flying onto the soaked grass. She really didn't feel much like brunch.

"Hurry," Beth urged. "Your food is getting cold."

"Okay." Cindy hesitated, then followed Beth into the B&B. She knew Beth wouldn't let up about eating properly in the morning.

Four small breakfast tables had been set up in the big dining area off the living room. Samantha and Ian were sitting at one table, sharing the newspaper.

Samantha looked up. "Good morning! Ready to do some sightseeing?"

"I guess so." Cindy managed an answering smile as she sat down next to her sister. She selected a croissant from the breadbasket. "But it's raining," she added.

Ian glanced at Cindy across the table. "Rain might mean an off track tomorrow," he said. "That would favor Glory."

"I know. So I hope it does keep raining." Cindy broke the delicious-looking homemade croissant in two and spread it with strawberry jam. She knew Glory liked to run in the mud. *But what if he doesn't go well for Kelly again?* she thought. It was all so frustrating. Cindy was sure that with the right kind of jockey, Glory could blow by the rest of the field in record time.

The outside door slammed. Cindy looked up and saw the dark-haired girl come in with her parents. That day she wore chocolate brown riding breeches, a tan and white striped T-shirt, and brown jodhpur boots. Her thick hair was held back with tortoiseshell clips. The girl ignored Cindy again as she sat at a table with her parents.

Look at those fancy clothes, Cindy thought. *How does she keep them so clean? She must never go near their horses.* Cindy didn't have to muck out stalls or groom the horses at Whitebrook, either—these days the farm could afford plenty of stable hands. But Cindy loved spending time with the horses, even if she was just talking to them or doing chores.

Beth looked over at the other table, too. "Why don't we ask Anne Tarin to come sightseeing with us?" she said. "That's Anne over there, Cindy. She's about your age. I thought we could go to an exhibit featuring horse art. I got acquainted with Anne's parents yesterday, and they seem very nice."

Oh, no, Cindy thought. *I'm going to have to be around Miss Stuck-up all day.* "I guess she can come," she said reluctantly. Cindy didn't think Anne seemed very nice, but she could tell Beth had already decided to ask her along.

Beth got up and approached the Tarins' table. Cindy heard a murmur of conversation, and Anne looked over at her. Anne narrowed her eyes.

Cindy scowled right back. She was adopted, and before she'd come to live with the McLeans, she'd been in a lot of tough foster homes. Nobody was going to intimidate her, whatever they thought of themselves.

"Everybody finished?" Beth asked, coming back over to the McLeans' table. Anne was right behind her.

"Yes." Cindy dropped her half-eaten croissant back on her plate.

"Cindy and Samantha, this is Anne," Beth introduced them.

"Hi, Anne," Ian said, smiling a welcome. "I hear your parents brought a couple of horses east for the fall Saratoga and Belmont meets."

"Yes, they did," Anne said. She was pretty even if she wasn't nice, Cindy decided. Anne had dark brown eyes the same color as her hair and an athletic build. *Maybe she's been on a horse after all,* Cindy thought.

"I never heard of the Tarins," Samantha said thoughtfully. "Of course, I'm not as familiar with West Coast trainers as I am with the East Coast ones."

Anne narrowed her eyes again. She seemed angry.

Now what's the matter with her? Cindy thought. She hoped Anne wasn't going to be moody or gripe all day. Cindy hated bad sports.

"Let's head out to the exhibit," Beth urged.

"Okay," Anne said, sounding as though she'd rather be tortured. Cindy rolled her eyes.

She and Samantha sat next to the backseat windows of the car, with Anne sandwiched between them. Cindy drew a pattern in the fog on her window and stared out at the glossy, rain-slick trees. Cindy's mind returned to the problem with Glory. *There must be some way to get him running the way he was,* she said to herself. *And I need to come up with it fast.*

Anne glanced sideways at her. "So you're March to Glory's groom."

"Yes," Cindy said proudly. "And I exercise-ride him when we're at home."

"We have some really good horses in our string, too," Anne said, sounding snobby.

"I never said you didn't." Cindy looked over at the other girl. Anne was staring straight ahead, her mouth tense. *I really wonder what her problem is,* Cindy thought.

"Here we are," Ian called, parking the car in front of a tall, modern glass building. Cindy walked quickly to avoid talking to Anne, but the other girl caught up.

"What's the matter?" Cindy asked bluntly. She might as well know. Maybe it would clear the air.

"I didn't want to come to New York." Anne sounded angry. "My friends are all in California. I wish my parents had stayed at Del Mar—most of the horses they train are there. But two are racing at Saratoga, so we had to come east with them."

"What horses do you have at the track?" Cindy asked politely. She thought Anne was acting unbelievably spoiled.

"Sensational Summer and Perfectly Fine—they're excellent allowance horses," Anne said proudly. "And our filly Dove into It will be running in the Nijana in a couple of days. That's a stakes race!"

"Neat," Cindy said carefully. The Nijana was only a grade-three stakes. Certainly the competition and prestige for running in that race were nothing like Shining's bid in the Whitney or Glory's run the next day in the Jim Dandy.

Anne scowled, obviously picking up on her tone. "I know, it's nothing to you. That's why I don't like being at Saratoga—everyone is so snobby."

"I'm not snobby!" Cindy protested. *Me snobby?* she thought in amazement. *Look who's talking!*

For the next hour Cindy followed her parents and Samantha around the art exhibit, glancing at the paintings and sculptures and trying to stay away from Anne. Cindy stopped in front of a marble sculpture of a running horse. In the smooth black stone the artist had captured the exquisite, flowing beauty of the Thoroughbred.

Cindy stared at the statue, seeing Glory. What would happen in the race the following day? Glory was probably in as much danger now as he had been when he'd run under the influence of drugs at Belmont. If the colt went badly under Kelly in the race, he could get hurt.

"So what's the matter with *you*?" Anne asked. "You're hardly looking at anything. I guess I'm not the only one who doesn't like it here."

"It's not that." Cindy shrugged. "I'm worried about my horse."

"March to Glory? He's the heavy favorite in the race tomorrow," Anne said in surprise.

"Yes, he is." Cindy didn't know Anne well enough to confide her fears about Glory. "I'm sure he'll win it," she said after a moment's hesitation.

Anne looked at her questioningly, but Cindy turned her attention back to the statue in front of them.

"Are you girls about ready to head for the track?" Ian called.

"Sure," Samantha answered as she crossed the room to join him and Beth.

It's going to be up to Glory how the race turns out tomorrow, Cindy thought as they hurried back to the car through the pelting rain. *Kelly can't really control him. I guess we just have to hope that Glory feels like running a good race.*

"Is Glory set?" Mike asked the next afternoon. Cindy looked up from grooming Glory as Mike, Samantha, and Ian walked toward them down the barn aisle. Cindy swallowed with nervousness and excitement. It was almost post time for the Jim Dandy.

"He's all ready." Cindy clipped a lead line to the colt's halter. She wasn't really sure if Glory was ready, after the way he had been acting, but she'd done all she could. She had brushed him for over an hour, and his dappled coat gleamed sleekly over rippling muscles. Physically Glory couldn't be more ready for his race. "Let's go, boy," she said.

Len walked over to stand on Glory's right side. He nodded encouragement to Cindy.

Glory nudged her cheerfully and moved out after her at a brisk walk. His long, silky mane and tail were gently ruffled by the cool breeze. The rain had stopped in the morning, but the fast-moving clouds were low and gray.

"He doesn't seem at all nervous," Samantha remarked.

"I know." Cindy wasn't sure if that was good or not. Probably it was good, she decided. Glory usually wasn't nervous before races. Maybe he was up to form.

39

"The track condition has been upgraded from sloppy to muddy," Mike said as they walked along the curving, tree-lined lane on the Saratoga backside. "It's still a mess out there, though."

Just ahead of them Cindy saw Adieu, a rangy black colt entered in the Jim Dandy, walking with his groom, trainer, and owner. Glory had raced Adieu in the Brooklyn Handicap in June, beating him by a wide margin. Cindy didn't think Adieu would pose much of a threat if Glory ran decently at all.

Suddenly Glory seemed to notice the other colt, too. He made a playful lunge at him. "Glory!" Cindy scolded, pulling the colt's head around. Glory danced in a circle, shifting his hindquarters sideways. "Settle down," Cindy warned, giving the lead line a little jerk. Glory stood still, but he blew out an excited snort.

"Are you doing all right?" Ian asked. He, Samantha, and Mike had walked ahead on the path.

"Yes!" Cindy said. Glory tossed his head and eyed her, but he followed her obediently again.

"Len, I'm so afraid he's going to fool around today," Cindy whispered.

"He might get fired up when he sees he's in an actual race," Len said. The stable manager smiled reassuringly at Cindy.

"Maybe." Cindy was beginning to doubt it, but she hoped Len was right.

In the saddling paddock Cindy smoothed onto Glory's back the saddlecloth in the blue-and-white colors of Whitebrook. Kelly walked over to join them.

"Take Glory right to the front," Ian told her. "But Adieu may try to force the pace. In that case, don't get caught in a killer speed duel—try to rate Glory in second or third."

"He doesn't mind mud in his face," Samantha commented.

Mike turned to Cindy. "Any ideas?" he asked.

"What?" Cindy was startled. Mike had never asked her for training advice before. "Not . . . not really," she said hesitantly. "I think Kelly just has to make him mind."

Mike frowned. "Well, try talking to him or whatever you usually do. I think we're going to need some of the magic you and Ashleigh work on him."

Cindy doubted her half of the magic would work without Ashleigh's half, but she had to try. She looked at Glory and stroked his neck. "Please run," she said. "Do it for me and Ashleigh, even though we can't be out there with you. I'll still love you even if you don't win—but it would be so great if you did!"

The colt rubbed the side of his head affectionately against her shoulder and sighed contentedly.

"I know," Cindy said. "We're best friends. But we're not out here to take it easy, Glory. You've got to do your best."

Len gave Kelly a leg into the small, light racing saddle. Glory craned his neck around and playfully bumped Kelly's boot with his head.

Cindy frowned. Glory still didn't seem to have his mind on business.

"Okay, let's go, Glory boy," Kelly said. She sounded optimistic. Cindy wasn't.

If only Ashleigh were here, Cindy thought for the thousandth time as she followed Mike, Samantha, and Ian to their seats in the grandstand. Cindy knew Glory better than anyone else, but Ashleigh had so much experience as a trainer. Cindy knew how to make Glory obey her, but she didn't have the experience to assess Glory's behavior and Kelly's abilities, then figure out how to put it all together so that Glory would run a good race for Kelly.

Beth was already sitting in their row. "Glory looks wonderful, honey," she said to Cindy.

Cindy looked out at the track. Glory was prancing excitedly, but Kelly was expertly guiding him in an arc around Superiority Complex, a gray New York–bred. *So far, so good,* Cindy thought hopefully.

The horses loaded into the gate. Even from a distance Cindy could hear muffled thumps as nine powerful colts shifted nervously in the narrow chutes, preparing for the sudden break.

The bell clanged, and Glory flew out of the gate, lithe muscle and beauty in motion. He quickly surged to the lead, churning up clods of mud behind him.

"Great break!" Samantha said excitedly.

"Perfect." Ian sat forward on his seat. "Glory's certainly handling the off going."

"Superiority Complex is challenging Glory for the lead." Mike sounded surprised. The other colt's jockey angled him in along the rail, saving ground and taking the lead.

"Watch out!" Cindy's hand flew to her mouth. Almost directly in front of Glory, Superiority Complex had slipped in the mud and fallen to his knees. Glory seemed sure to plow into the fallen horse!

But at the last possible moment Glory changed leads and darted around the struggling colt. He pounded ahead, splashing nimbly through puddles. Behind him the other horses were already gray-brown with splattered mud.

"Glory didn't miss a stride!" Ian said.

"I know!" Cindy was breathless. The horses thundered around the clubhouse turn with Glory in the lead by two lengths. "You're the greatest, Glory!" Cindy screamed. "Just keep going like that and you'll win it!"

"I think Superiority's jockey had to try to take the lead," Samantha shouted above the roar of the crowd as the muddy horse and jockey continued on in the race, lengths behind the rest of the field. "Superiority doesn't like being rated or having mud in his face."

"And it's March to Glory in the lead by three lengths," the announcer called. "Adieu is in second, Good Night to All in third . . . "

Glory was running effortlessly, maintaining his lead. Several horses were struggling with the muddy going. Adieu slid sideways almost into the rail as the field came out of the turn, nearly unseating his jockey. But Glory's strides were even and sure as he plowed through the mud on the backstretch.

Still, Glory usually opened up a big lead in a

trouble-free race like this one had been for him, Cindy thought. Adieu had come back from his near collision with the rail and was pressing at Glory's flank. Good Night to All was two lengths back. He seemed to be laboring in the mud, but he wasn't giving up. Cindy felt uneasy as the horses swept around the far turn.

"March to Glory is falling behind!" the announcer called. "He may be injured!"

Cindy gasped and stood up, trying to see if Glory was favoring one of his legs. She felt Beth and Samantha rise next to her.

"Is Kelly trying to pull him up?" Samantha asked.

"No." Ian adjusted his binoculars. "He's still in contention. I don't see anything wrong with his stride."

Cindy looked closely at Glory through her own binoculars. He dropped back to second behind Adieu, then third behind Good Night to All as the field roared into the stretch. She recognized the bounce to Glory's stride. "He's playing around!" Cindy gasped.

"Kelly has to stop that," Ian said grimly.

"I don't believe it!" Beth cried.

Cindy could hardly stand to watch. Glory was galloping gaily along, barely exerting himself. *If he would put in half an effort, he'd win by thirty lengths*, she thought unhappily.

"Make him extend!" Mike yelled.

Cindy knew what he meant. When Glory was putting out a real effort in a race, his head was almost level with his tail as he stretched for ground. But that day he was loafing along like a rocking horse. Mike looked as frustrated as Cindy felt.

The field whipped by the quarter pole. Cindy squeezed her hands into fists. The race was almost over, and Glory was in third and still losing ground. He was running out of time!

Suddenly Glory seemed to realize that he might lose. He tugged sharply on the reins. Adieu and Good Night to All were squarely in front of him, and Cindy saw Kelly check the colt hard to avoid running over them.

But Glory was having none of it. He angled out from the rail and began to go two wide to pass the other horses.

Cindy could hardly believe Glory's acceleration. A gray and brown streak, he raced by Good Night to All and bore down on Adieu. "Come on, Glory!" she screamed. "Catch him!"

Mike groaned. "He can't do it."

Glory powered up on Adieu's flank, reaching for ground. Glory's gray head moved steadily up to Adieu's shoulder, then the horses were almost head to head. The two colts flashed under the wire.

"And March to Glory rallies late to finish second by a nose!" the announcer called.

Cindy shook her head. She felt sick with disappointment. Glory had never lost a race before, except when he was disqualified for drugging that wasn't his fault. This was a disaster.

"I don't know about the Breeders' Cup now," Ian

said with a sigh as they headed out of the stands to the track. "We've got the Travers in just three weeks, but if today is any indication, Glory may be over-matched in a grade-one race."

Beth squeezed Cindy's shoulder.

"I think Glory can beat the Travers field. And after that there are still some more races to go before the Breeders' Cup," Samantha said quickly.

Cindy managed a smile. That was true, but she was afraid Glory's career was spoiled anyway. Cindy hadn't told anyone but Ben that she had higher goals for Glory than winning the Breeders' Cup Classic. She hoped he'd go down in the history books as one of the greatest racehorses of all time, like his grand-sire Just Victory. Just Victory's records still stood at many of the major tracks.

But at this rate Glory would be lucky to qualify for the Breeders' Cup, Cindy thought as Kelly brought the colt over to them. And even if he did, Ashleigh wouldn't be riding. Glory might perform worse than he had that day.

Glory was covered with mud, and his sides were heaving. Cindy reached for his reins, quickly examining him. He seemed tired but not exhausted. He would probably be fine after a sponge bath and a long walk.

Kelly dismounted. She was covered with mud, too, and trying to catch her breath.

"What happened out there?" Ian asked. His voice was quiet, but Cindy could tell that he was angry.

Kelly shrugged miserably. "He broke well, and

then I thought we had it at the end. I couldn't get his attention during most of the ride. You told me not to even show him the whip."

"Glory . . ." Cindy looked at the colt unhappily. She could feel tears pressing in her eyes and began quickly to lead him to the backside. There was nothing to hang around for—Glory wouldn't be going in the winner's circle. And Cindy didn't really want to hear Kelly being scolded. She was sure the jockey had done her best.

"We'll be there in a second, Cindy," Mike called.

Glory lowered his head and followed Cindy obediently on a loose lead. *I wonder if he feels bad about losing,* she thought. She knew that sometimes when racehorses lost, it affected their spirits so badly they had trouble running again.

Behind them she heard the sticky clopping of hooves in the mud. "We lost because of the track," she heard Superiority Complex's jockey say ruefully.

"You don't have that excuse, do you, Glory?" Cindy asked her horse. "You could have won if you'd tried a little sooner." Glory loved mud. At home he played in puddles and rolled in them.

That was exactly what he had done in the race, she realized—gone out on the track and played in the mud. He hadn't run a race until the last quarter mile.

He did rally at the end, she thought as she led Glory toward the barn for a quick sponging. *Maybe he won't make the same mistake next time.*

Cindy shook her head. Glory was a smart horse, but he needed a jockey to give him opportunities and cues. He couldn't run a race by himself and win. That was what had happened just now.

Cindy glanced down the barn aisle and saw Brad and Lavinia Townsend standing in front of Glory's stall. Cindy felt her stomach lurch. Brad and Lavinia always made snide remarks about Whitebrook's horses. Cindy knew she couldn't stand to hear that kind of thing right then, on top of her disappointment about Glory.

"Not a bad race," Brad remarked, stepping closer to the colt. "He seems to have come out of it all right." Cindy stared at Brad in amazement.

"March to Glory just needs a better jockey," Lavinia agreed, smiling.

Mike and Ian walked down the barn aisle. Cindy was glad to see them. She knew she was no match for the Townsends.

"Glory's performance was disappointing," Mike said stiffly. Cindy knew he could barely hide his dislike for Brad and Lavinia.

"Glory finished the last eighth in eleven seconds flat in the mud," Brad said. His handsome face was thoughtful. "That's really moving."

"Well, he still couldn't close." Ian sighed.

Brad and Lavinia never said anything nice about Glory even when he won, Cindy thought, protectively leading the colt away from them to sponge him. *What's going on? I'm sure it's nothing good.*

4

"Easy does it, Sagebrush," Cindy said the next day as she and Samantha carefully loaded the injured horse into the trailer for the long trip home to Kentucky. Samantha, Cindy, and Mike planned to drive back Sagebrush, a two-year-old in the Whitebrook string, so that the bone chip in the chestnut colt's knee could be treated. They would also collect Four Leaf Clover for the selected yearling sale and Sierra for the big New York Turf Writers Steeplechase at Saratoga and be back in a few days.

Limping slightly, Sagebrush walked up the ramp behind Samantha with Cindy gently urging him from behind. As the colt loaded, Cindy frowned critically at the heavy travel bandages encasing Sagebrush's legs. She and Samantha had spent an hour that morning carefully adjusting the bandages. The track vet had said the trailer ride wouldn't hurt Sagebrush as long as his legs were protected.

"I'm going to say good-bye to Glory." Cindy shut

the trailer door behind Sagebrush after Samantha hopped off the ramp. The colt was contentedly chomping the hay Cindy had put in his net.

Samantha laughed. "You already said good-bye to Glory all day yesterday and again after his gallop this morning! Come on, Cindy. It's almost afternoon. We need to hit the road—we've got a long drive ahead of us."

"I know. I'll just be a second." Cindy was already walking quickly toward the Whitebrook shed row.

As she approached the barn, Shining, Matchless, and the five other horses stabled on the row looked over their doors and whinnied or nickered. Glory had his head the farthest out. He whinnied loudly with delight. Probably he hoped she had come to let him out.

"Not today, boy," Cindy said, reaching up to push back his thick forelock. "I'm going home for a little while."

She felt an ache in her chest at the thought of leaving her beloved colt, even for just a few days. She particularly hated to leave him when he was in trouble.

Glory's next race was in just three weeks. Earlier that morning Glory had put in a so-so work for another jockey Ian was trying, but Cindy had seen that the colt's heart wasn't in it.

Glory nodded briskly, still trying to convey that he would like to be let out of the stall.

Cindy took the colt's head between her hands. "No, we're not going anywhere," she said. "Look, Glory.

You just have to snap out of it. Nobody's going to do it for you. You saw what happened in your last race."

Glory eyed her, then wrested his head away with a snort.

"I know, you don't think you're doing anything wrong," Cindy said with a sigh. "But you are, Glory. You're blowing your chance to be famous."

Glory gave her a rude shove with his nose, as if to say, *I don't appreciate the criticism.*

Cindy laughed, then gave him a last pat. "Be good," she warned.

As she walked back to the truck, Cindy remembered she had heard that Flightful, Joe Gallagher's horse, had recently won a big stakes race at Hollywood Park. Flightful was accumulating a lot of points and was definitely in contention for the Breeders' Cup. If Glory didn't settle down and win his next race, he definitely *wouldn't* be.

I'll see Ashleigh tomorrow, Cindy thought. *Maybe she'll have some ideas.*

Samantha and Mike were already waiting inside the truck. Beth and Ian stood nearby to see them all off.

"Don't forget to brush your teeth!" Beth reminded Cindy as she climbed into the backseat. "And don't eat fast food for every meal!"

"Do what Sammy tells you!" Ian called.

"Bye, Mom and Dad!" Cindy yelled, not answering their admonitions. Mike honked a farewell. As they drove through town he took the turns carefully so that Sagebrush wouldn't lose his balance. Cindy still heard the occasional thump as the colt struggled to keep his footing. Minutes later they reached the highway.

Samantha turned around in the front seat. "So you'd better mind me, Cindy," she said with a fierce scowl. "We're going to have some strict rules around here."

"Okay," Cindy said with a laugh. She knew Samantha was just joking. Cindy glanced excitedly out the window at the lush green countryside rolling by. She was already having a blast. It was great to be away from fussing parents and the pressures of the track. "How far do we have to get tonight?"

"I made reservations at a horse motel in Pittsburgh, Pennsylvania," Samantha answered. "Sagebrush has a stall near our rooms. That way he can get out of the trailer and relax."

"We'll stop for a burger as soon as we get out of town," Mike said, expertly navigating through traffic. "I want to see if Sagebrush is holding up all right."

"But Beth made us turkey sandwiches," Cindy reminded him. She looked out the back window of the truck. She could see Sagebrush through the tinted glass of the small front trailer window. He was bouncing around some, but he seemed to have one big brown eye fixed on her.

"We'll eat Beth's sandwiches later. Burgers and fries are real road food." Mike glanced briefly in the rearview mirror and winked at Cindy.

"I'd love a burger," she said cheerfully.

"Burgers all around." Mike took the next exit and pulled into a truck stop.

"I hope the fries are really greasy and disgusting." Samantha grinned. "Let's order three plates."

That night in the motel Cindy picked up the movie listing from on top of the big-screen TV. She saw that an action movie featuring her favorite male star would start in ten minutes.

Holding the channel changer, Cindy lay back on her king-size bed, plumping two pillows behind her head. "What movie do you want to watch, Sammy?" she asked.

Her older sister stood in front of the window across the room, looking out into the night. Samantha didn't answer or even seem to hear.

Cindy got up and went over to stand beside her. "Sammy, are you all right?" she asked.

Samantha started, then smiled uncertainly at her. "Sure," she said. But Cindy saw tears in her eyes.

"What were you thinking?" Cindy looked out the window, too. Their room was on the top floor of the motel. Far below, the sparkling white and red lights of the city and traffic swept across the black night.

"I was just thinking about this city. I've been here before, a long time ago. Dad, my mother, and I were on our way to the Arlington track in Illinois to run some claimers." Samantha's voice was sad.

"You used to travel a lot, didn't you?" Cindy asked. She wondered why her sister seemed so pensive.

"Almost all the time when I was your age."

53

Samantha pressed her face gently to the cool glass, as if she were searching for something in the darkness. "Dad was still training claimers, and he and Mom and I traveled around the country to different small tracks all year. We really weren't based anywhere, although I was born in Florida. It wasn't a bad life—we were so happy together. Until that one morning . . . when my mother was killed. I was twelve."

"She was killed in a riding accident, right?" Cindy asked sympathetically.

"Yes. I was right there when it happened." Samantha closed her eyes. "It was the most terrible thing I've ever seen. The green horse she was exercising went through a fence. One second she was alive, and the next . . . her neck was broken, and she was dead. I was the first to get to her." Samantha was silent for several moments. "I just couldn't believe it wasn't all a nightmare."

"I'm really sorry, Sammy," Cindy said softly. She could see that even after six years, Samantha was still upset about her mother's death.

"Dad was heartbroken," Samantha said. "Just before the accident, he'd finally begun to make it big as a trainer. A horse we were running had won the Donn Handicap, and we were planning to stay for good near Gulfstream Park in Florida. But then Dad started moving around again, as if he couldn't stand to have a home." Samantha wiped her eyes.

"That's what I always wanted more than any-thing—a home," Cindy said.

Samantha squeezed her hand. "I know. Here I am

feeling sorry for myself, and you've had it way rougher than I ever did."

"I guess." Cindy gazed out into the starless night again. She had never known her parents—they had died in a car accident, killed by a drunk driver, when she was a baby. *Maybe that's better than missing them all the time,* she thought. But after her parents' death, she'd spent the next ten years shuttling from one miserable, uncaring foster home to the next until the McLeans had adopted her six months earlier, when she was eleven. Intensely happy with her new parents and life around the horses, Cindy seldom thought about the bad times in the past.

"Well, one door closes and another one opens," Samantha said, as if she'd read Cindy's mind. "I like Beth so much. And it's wonderful what she's done for Dad. He's a happy, new person since she came into his life."

"Beth's pretty amazing," Cindy agreed. "I couldn't ask for a nicer mom. And Ashleigh and Mike are so great, too. I feel like their baby is part of our family."

"That baby's going to have a lot of aunts," Samantha agreed. "So . . ." She turned decisively from the window. "That's enough moping, don't you think? Thanks for listening, Cindy."

"You're welcome," Cindy said shyly. Samantha had given her lots of advice in the past. She'd even convinced their dad and Mike that Glory was worth buying at auction by riding him before Whitebrook owned him. She could have gotten in a lot of trouble for that. Cindy was glad she could do something for Samantha in return.

"Let's watch one of those movies!" Samantha grinned. "That's as obligatory as eating greaseburgers when you're on the road."

Cindy jumped back on her bed and flicked on the TV. The great action movie she'd wanted to see filled the large screen. Cindy snuggled between the starched, clean-smelling sheets to watch. She felt excited about spending the night away from her parents, sleepy from the long drive, and contented all at once. Looked at from a distance, even the situation with Glory seemed bearable.

No matter what happens, I've got my family and friends behind me, she thought. *Together we'll figure out what to do about Glory.*

"You know what?" she said to Samantha. Her older sister was just picking up the phone. In her other hand she held the room service menu.

"What?" Samantha put down the receiver.

"I'm so glad I came to Whitebrook," Cindy said simply.

Samantha smiled warmly. "Me, too. I couldn't be happier that you're my sister."

5

The next day at dusk Mike pulled the truck into the gravel driveway at Whitebrook. "We're home!" he said. "Man, it's good to be back!"

Cindy jumped out of the truck and looked around, relishing the sight of the farm after her two months in New York. The twilight had touched the big red-painted training barn and the smaller mares' and stallions' barns, turning them dusky maroon. The McLeans' white cottage, Len's smaller cottage near the barns, and Ashleigh and Mike's classic two-hundred-year-old farmhouse were tinged with blue as the light slowly left the horizon.

Cindy let out a long, happy sigh. She fully agreed with Mike. No matter how thrilling life was on the road, it always felt wonderful to be home. They would be leaving again in two days—they were staying only long enough for Mike to be sure the stable was in order and to pick up Sierra and Clover—but being home was a welcome break,

Cindy thought. Glory's race was in over two weeks. She'd have plenty of time to be with him before then.

Out in the big front paddock were the fifteen mares with their foals. Vic Teleski and Mark Collier, Whitebrook's full-time grooms, had left the horses out longer than usual in the exquisite summer evening. Cindy spotted Wonder hungrily grazing the lush, damp grass near the back fence. For a second Cindy didn't see Wonder's Champion. Then she spotted the dark chestnut colt galloping around the fence line, as if he were exercising himself.

"I'm going up to the house to check the messages on the answering machine," Samantha said to Mike and Cindy. "I'll meet you at the barns in a few minutes."

Mike nodded. "I'll take care of Sagebrush, then I'll be in the office."

"I'll be out here." Cindy was already walking quickly to the paddocks to see the horses.

"Welcome back!" Vic called from near the mares' paddock. He had several halters and lead ropes slung over his shoulder. "Want to help me bring them in?"

"You bet!" Cindy took a lead rope and halter from Vic and opened the gate. She thought she'd have to cross the paddock to collect the horses—sometimes they didn't want to leave the tasty grass to come in— but Wonder's Champion was already trotting her way. With a loud whinny the beautiful colt glided up to the fence. Already he was the picture of grace and breeding.

"You didn't forget me!" Cindy said with a laugh. "And you've gotten so big and gorgeous."

Cindy ran her hand down the colt's short, full mane. Wonder's Champion took a step closer, clearly enjoying the attention. He was already fearless around people, Cindy thought. That would be a plus when he went into training. She only wished Glory had been treated well earlier in his life. If he had, they might not have a lot of the problems they had with him now.

Stroking the colt's velvety neck, Cindy gazed at the mile training oval behind the barns, where she had so often galloped Glory. And in just over a year Wonder's Champion would begin yearling training there.

The colt looked at the track, too.

"Hmmm," Cindy said. "Do you think we might be out there someday riding together? I'll bet Ashleigh will let me exercise-ride you next year." Cindy gazed into the soft gray light of the deepening twilight. She almost thought she could see herself and the elegant colt floating around the oval. And after that she could ride him at Churchill Downs and other big tracks.

It would be a dream come true to ride a horse of that caliber at the track, Cindy thought. She'd never be able to ride Glory in a race—when she was sixteen, he'd be seven and probably retired to stud. But riding Wonder's Champion in races was a real possibility. He'd be just four when she was sixteen.

"And if I rode you all along, starting next year, I'd really be ready," Cindy murmured.

But none of that would happen if the Townsends

took the colt. Cindy rubbed her arms, suddenly chilled in the approaching night.

They couldn't take him, she decided. Wonder's Champion was too sweet and talented to be ruined. She was sure Ashleigh would come up with a way to keep him at Whitebrook.

Wonder and the other mares and foals were slowly moving toward the gate, anticipating the evening feeding. Cindy shook off her good and bad daydreams. She had to get the horses in. She'd start with Wonder and Wonder's Champion, since they were the first to the gate.

As she led the willing mare and foal to the barn, Cindy could see where Wonder's Champion had gotten his good looks. Wonder was eleven, but her classic, finely sculpted head, slender, well-angled legs, and gleaming copper coat were as beautiful as ever. She wasn't in foal for the next year. Mike, Ashleigh, and Mr. Townsend had decided to give her a rest, over the strenuous objections of Lavinia Townsend.

Suddenly Wonder's Champion caught sight of Mark, Whitebrook's new young groom, holding a feed bucket in the brightly lit doorway of the mares' barn. Just before they left for Saratoga, Mike and Ian had hired Mark to help with the growing workload at Whitebrook. Also Mike's father, Gene Reese, had been ill for some time. He was unable to take the active part in running the stable that he had in the past.

The foal charged ahead. "Settle down!" Cindy called, quickly pulling his head around.

Wonder's Champion stopped, but he planted all four feet and continued to strain against the lead.

"I'm going to get mad if you don't cut it out," Cindy warned as she and Wonder caught up with him. "I know you want to go in. But you just have to be patient."

Wonder's Champion shook his small head, then arched his neck and pranced after her. He seemed to be saying, *Well, at least you know I won't be pushed around.*

As Cindy shut the two horses in their stall, she thought that Wonder's Champion was another horse that would need the right rider. He looked bigger and sturdier than most of Wonder's offspring. That might be good; they'd had problems with the soundness of Wonder and her other foals.

But what will really count is if he has her speed and heart, Cindy thought as she watched Wonder eagerly tear off a mouthful of hay.

Cindy went back out to the side paddock to get Four Leaf Clover, now a yearling. The dark chestnut colt was lined up at the fence with the five other yearlings, including his twin brother, Rainbow.

"You look wonderful, boy," Cindy said with a smile as she buckled on his halter. "How did you get so big?" It seemed much longer than a year since she'd had to bottle-feed him and Rainbow, right after they were born and she'd first come to Whitebrook. Twin foals were usually very weak, and for months no one knew if Clover and Rainbow would live.

Cindy looked at the colt a moment. Clover was

here now, big and beautiful and affectionate. But in just two days they'd take him to Saratoga, and a short time after that he'd be auctioned off.

I should be glad, she reminded herself. *The Saratoga sale is for excellent horses. And Clover came so close to not making it at all.*

In the training barn Cindy latched the stall door behind Clover and turned to leave. By now Mark had brought all the other horses in, and she could go up to the house. Samantha was ordering a pizza for dinner, and Cindy wanted to make sure part of it came with her favorite toppings—pepperoni and green peppers.

I'll just say good night to Princess, she thought. *Princess deserves a special visit, since she's still hurt.*

As she walked down the aisle Cindy's eye fell on Glory's empty stall at the middle of the barn. Her buoyant mood evaporated, and she felt a sharp pang of loneliness. What was Glory doing? she wondered. Was he eating or just standing in his stall? Did he miss her as much as she missed him?

But Cindy saw that the stall wasn't quite empty. Imp, the gray calico cat who had adopted Glory, was pacing up and down on top of the stall door.

"Poor guy," Cindy said, running her hand along the cat's back. "Do you miss your friend?" Glory and Imp had been inseparable since Glory had first come to Whitebrook. Even their dappled coat colors matched.

The young cat arched his back and fervently rubbed against Cindy's shoulder. "Glory will be back," Cindy promised. "This winter at the latest."

And I really hope no sooner, even though I miss him, she thought as she headed to Princess's stall. She knew if Glory lost his next couple of races, he'd be back in no time.

"Hey, Cindy!" Ashleigh greeted her from in front of Princess's stall. The beautiful filly had her head over the door and was eagerly lipping up carrots from Ashleigh's hands.

"Hi!" Cindy ran over to join her. Ashleigh still didn't look pregnant, she noticed with disappointment.

"I know, I'm still pretty thin," Ashleigh said with a laugh, following Cindy's glance. "But I don't think I will be for long—I'm eating twice as much as usual. Anyway, I *feel* pregnant."

Princess leaned farther over the stall door and urgently poked Ashleigh's hands with her muzzle, as if to say, *Don't forget me.*

"How is Princess?" Cindy asked. She always hated to ask, because the news was never very good. That Princess was alive was an ongoing miracle, she knew. But before the filly had gotten hurt, she'd been slated to run in the Kentucky Derby.

"She's still hanging in there." Ashleigh looked over Princess with a critical eye. "She's holding her weight pretty well. We may be able to breed her next spring, but I'm not counting on it."

"When do you think Mr. Wonderful can run again?" Cindy asked. Wonder's two-year-old son had strained a tendon in the spring.

Ashleigh frowned. "I'm not sure. I'd really hoped

he'd be at Belmont this fall for the Champagne stakes, but that's starting to look more and more like a distant possibility. We might campaign him in Florida this winter."

"Let's go look at Wonder's Champion," Cindy suggested. Suddenly Ashleigh seemed so down, she thought. Maybe seeing Wonder's healthy son would get Ashleigh's mind off all the uncertainty and misfortune associated with the mare's other offspring.

"Good idea." Ashleigh smiled. "You wouldn't believe how high my hopes for him are already."

The dark chestnut colt was sleeping, stretched flat out beside Wonder. With a throaty whicker the mare put her head over the stall door.

"Hi, girl," Ashleigh whispered. "Aren't you the most special horse ever?"

Wonder's Champion instantly started awake. As if he couldn't stand to be outdone by his mother, the sleep-drunk foal tottered to the half-door and stuck his muzzle almost straight up, trying to reach over the door and get their attention.

"I'm still having it out with the Townsends about him," Ashleigh said, rubbing the whiskery tip of the colt's muzzle. "I know I'm just as greedy as they are. I want all Wonder's offspring here."

"Yeah, but that's because you care about them," Cindy argued. "The Townsends usually ruin them." Then she regretted her words because Ashleigh looked so pained.

"Well, I have to be realistic," Ashleigh said with a

sigh. "The Townsends and I are in this together. I can't have things all my way."

"I guess not." Cindy still didn't think the Townsends were ever fair to Ashleigh or the horses they co-owned with her.

"Tell me about Glory," Ashleigh said. "I talked to Mike yesterday, but I'd like to get the complete picture from you."

Cindy hesitated. She didn't want to make Ashleigh feel that she'd let Glory down, but the fact remained that he just wouldn't run for anybody but her.

"Tell me the truth," Ashleigh urged. "We can't solve this unless I know what's really going on."

Cindy took a deep breath. "Well, Glory's getting worse and worse. I think acting up is a habit now—he's done it every time he's worked, and he did it in his last race."

"I'm sure you're right." Ashleigh kicked the tip of her boot thoughtfully against the boards of the stall. "I'll keep working on it," she promised. "Don't worry, Cindy. I really think this sounds worse than it is. I know a lot of jockeys—someone must be right for Glory. Maybe we can get the situation straightened out before the Travers."

"But you won't be at the track to see what he's doing," Cindy said, feeling panicky again. If Glory didn't win his next race—the Travers, a big one—his chance of going to the Breeders' Cup would be virtually gone.

"I don't know if it matters whether I'm there,"

Ashleigh said. "I know Glory pretty well, and you'll keep me posted. Besides, I'll be back at Saratoga about a week before the Travers."

Cindy felt better as she and Ashleigh walked out of the barn together. *If anyone can figure out what to do about Glory, it's Ashleigh,* she thought.

6

"Who let Sierra out?" Cindy cried early the next morning as she raced to the side paddock. She had just finished cleaning out the last stall in the training barn and had caught a glimpse through the open barn door of Sierra, cavorting in the wrong paddock.

"Oh, no!" Samantha and Tor, who had both just gotten out of Tor's car, rushed toward Sierra, too. Samantha stopped only to grab a halter and lead rope off the fence of the mares' paddock.

Sierra was circling the side paddock at a leisurely gallop, letting out small snorts of pleasure with each stride.

"I put him in there," Mark said, hurrying after them. The groom looked puzzled. "What's the matter? He's just kicking up his heels."

"He's going to kick them up right over that fence," Samantha said, panting as she opened the paddock gate. "Sierra!"

The liver chestnut stallion ignored her. He continued to circle, going slightly faster.

Cindy knew Sierra well enough to agree heartily with Samantha that he was about to make his escape. Sierra was capable of easily taking six-foot jumps, and the fences around most of the paddocks were only five feet.

The two exercise horses in the paddock with Sierra were standing under a tree together, watching as if they were enjoying the show. They also seemed to be staying out of the way.

Sierra stopped at the far end of the paddock, well out of Samantha's reach, and tossed his head. Sierra still hadn't acknowledged the humans' presence with so much as a look in their direction.

Cindy watched the wayward stallion, torn between worry and amusement.

"He doesn't even have a halter on," Tor said.

"I took it off after I let him out. I didn't want him to hang himself up on something." Mark sounded worried.

"It's okay." Samantha stared out at Sierra and sighed. "You couldn't have known. Sierra's too smart to hang himself up. And without a halter—"

"He can be extremely hard to catch," Tor finished. "Also, Sierra should go out only in the back paddock. Mike raised the fence there to six feet. Sierra *could* jump that, too, but usually he doesn't bother. As it is, I think he's getting ready to jump out."

"I'll try to catch him," Mark said determinedly.

"No, let Sammy—" Tor began. But Mark was already walking across the deep grass.

Mark advanced on the stallion. Sierra stood calmly. He quickly dropped his head to grab a mouthful of grass.

"Maybe Sierra thinks it's feeding time and he *will* let Mark catch him," Samantha murmured.

"I doubt it," Tor said.

Mark made a grab for Sierra's neck with the lead rope.

"No!" Tor and Samantha cried at the same time.

It was too late. Sierra lightly lifted his front legs and wheeled out of reach of his pursuer. The next moment he was galloping headlong for the fence. Sierra gathered his legs beneath him and glided over the five-foot fence, landing in the adjoining paddock. He galloped on, tossing his head and snorting, obviously delighted with his performance.

Cindy stared after the vanishing horse in frustration. Sierra's strides were lengthening as he enthusiastically galloped on. He seemed to be enjoying the cool early morning wind and the feel of the damp ground underfoot.

Samantha sighed. "I hope he doesn't get in trouble," she said.

"I'm sorry." Mark sounded worried.

"Don't be—someone should have told you about Sierra." Samantha managed a smile. "Sierra's done this before. He'll just go down the road to the next farm and jump the fence to get in with their horses. Luckily they're all geldings. We just have to go get him at the Marshalls' and apologize for the umpteenth time." She looked at Tor. "You were just about to exercise him. I guess Sierra did his own exercise today."

"That's what he thinks." Tor was already heading for his car. "On the way back we're going to take some fences."

"Let's go get him right now," Samantha said. "We shouldn't let him run loose." Cindy heard the note of anxiety in Samantha's voice and understood the reason. Sierra was an extremely valuable horse. He might be a terror on the ground, but with a rider up he was one of the best steeplechasers in the country.

Samantha and Tor loaded Sierra's tack in Tor's car. Cindy walked back up to the house to call Max. She was still concerned about Sierra, but Samantha and Tor seemed to have the situation under control.

Cindy had stayed out too late at the barn the night before to call anyone, but she was eager to talk to Max. He loved to hear about the Whitebrook horses, especially Glory. *I could use a friend to talk to*, she thought.

Cindy picked up the hall phone and dialed the Smiths' number.

Max answered on the first ring. "Hello?"

"Hi, it's Cindy! We're back."

Max pretended to think. "Cindy who? Oh, *Glory's* Cindy. *That* one. How have you been?"

Cindy laughed. "Very funny. I've been fine."

"But how's Glory?" Max asked. "I wondered what happened, because he lost the Jim Dandy. . . ."

Cindy hesitated. "I'll tell you later," she said finally. She found it difficult to talk about her beloved colt's failure. "So, what are you doing today?"

"Nothing. My mom's out on an emergency call. You could come over," Max suggested. "We can go for a ride."

Cindy had been planning to ride one of Whitebrook's exercise horses. "Or you could come over here."

"I have to wait for my mom to get back," Max said. "Besides, if you come here, we can ride Western."

Cindy was curious what that would be like. No one at Whitebrook rode Western, although at the different tracks she had seen that a lot of the escort riders were up on Western saddles. "Okay," she said. "Sammy could probably bring me over." Cindy thought a moment. "I think I can be there at about noon. If I can't, I'll call you back."

"Sounds good," Max said.

Cindy hung up, then quickly picked up the phone to call Heather. She hadn't talked to her best friend in weeks. Ian and Beth had forbidden Cindy to make long-distance calls after she had lost track of the time and talked to Heather for over an hour from Belmont.

"Cindy, it's so great to talk to you!" Heather said excitedly when she picked up.

"Same here. How've you been?" Cindy thought it was wonderful to hear Heather's voice. Her friend was only a quarter of a mile away.

"I've been really good. I've got my jumping lesson this afternoon at Tor's," Heather said. "Do you want to come watch?"

"Sure!" *Perfect,* Cindy thought. *I'll get to see all my friends right away.* "Could we go to the mall before your lesson?" she asked. "I need to buy Ashleigh and Mike a present."

"Why? Are you just being nice?"

"Not exactly." Cindy drew a deep breath. "They're having a baby!"

"Oh, wow! How exciting!" Heather was silent for a second. "But that means Ashleigh won't be riding Glory, right?"

"Yeah. And he's not too happy about it." Cindy decided not to get into the details.

"Well, do you want to meet at the mall?" Heather asked.

"How about at two o'clock in front of Rayson's?" Cindy said, naming one of the big department stores at the mall.

"Okay. I'll call Mandy and see if she can come, too. We'll see you then." Heather hung up.

Cindy was glad that Heather was inviting Mandy to join them. Mandy boarded her pony, Butterball, at Tor's stable and took jumping lessons from him. Despite her leg braces, the result of a car accident when she was five, the spunky eight-year-old was very accomplished at jumping.

"I'll drive you around," Samantha offered when she heard Cindy's plans. "I have to go down to the university and check on my schedule for next semester anyway. I could drop you off at the Smiths' on my way into town. Just let me get my keys."

"Thanks, Sammy," Cindy said gratefully. "I guess you caught Sierra?"

"Red-handed, you might say. He was having a second breakfast at the Marshalls'." Samantha shook her head. "He just shouldered one of their horses aside and dug in. Tor rode him back, but he couldn't really pound him over fences the way he'd wanted to because Sierra was full of food. If I didn't know better, I'd say Sierra planned the whole thing. So, are you about ready to go?"

"I just need to get my boots." Cindy didn't have the traditional Western riding attire of chaps, cowboy boots, and a cowboy hat, but she figured her low English jodhpur boots and jeans would do.

At the Smiths' small farm Samantha pulled up in front of their ranch-style house. Max was already walking toward Cindy down the drive. "Thanks, Sammy," Cindy said as she got out of the car.

"See you later," Samantha called. Cindy heard the scrunch of tires on the drive as Samantha drove away.

"Hey, Cindy!" Max waved and hurried over to join her. "Ready to ride?"

"You bet." A flashy paint in the front paddock caught Cindy's eye. The horse had big brown patches on satiny white and a black mane and tail. "Who's that guy?" she asked, walking to the fence.

Max grinned. "He's *your* guy—if you want to ride him. That's Gold Rush."

"I guess I can't get anything superfast around here," Cindy joked. "No Thoroughbreds."

"Wait till you see how fast a Quarter Horse can move," Max said. "Gold Rush is a barrel racer."

Cindy knew that barrel racing was a Western rodeo event in which the horse was timed running around three barrels. At the higher levels it was very competitive.

Gold Rush walked over to the fence, as if he sensed they were talking about him. Cindy noted the gelding's bunchy shoulder muscles and hindquarters. He looked built for quick speed. He was probably a little over fifteen hands, shorter than most Thoroughbreds.

"I thought Gold Rush was a paint." Cindy patted Gold Rush's white muzzle. She knew paints were a specific breed with their own registry.

"He's registered as both a paint and a Quarter Horse." Max opened the gate and expertly haltered Gold Rush. "So I'll go get Dynamite while you tack up Gold Rush. Then we'll be ready to ride."

"I can't wait!"

Cindy led Gold Rush up to the Smiths' ten-stall barn while Max went to get his Thoroughbred, Dynamite. The barn was cool and dim after the bright sunshine outside.

Cindy crosstied the paint and found a box of brushes in front of the stall with Gold Rush's nameplate on it. Gold Rush's sleek summer coat hardly needed brushing. The paint stood quietly as she groomed him, occasionally rolling a big brown eye back to look at her. He seemed very intelligent, Cindy decided. But he was much calmer than the Thoroughbreds she was used to—even Glory.

Max returned with Dynamite, a chestnut gelding, and crosstied him facing Gold Rush.

"Dynamite's a beautiful horse," Cindy said, examining him closely. She had never seen Max's horse before. Gold Rush looked even more muscular and short compared to the rangy Thoroughbred.

"Thanks," Max replied. "I've had him for two years. My mom bought him at a claiming race. He'd been racing in allowance races, but he fractured a splint bone. My mom operated to take out a piece of bone. He's been sound ever since."

"What's the emergency your mom is treating?" Cindy asked. She liked to listen to Dr. Smith, Max's mother, talk about the patients in her veterinary practice. Cindy had ambitions to be a vet herself—and a jockey, too.

"Colic," Max called from the tack room. He emerged carrying a beautiful Western saddle and set it down beside Gold Rush.

Cindy's eyes widened as she took in the intricate detail of the hand-tooled leatherwork. The dark saddle with its matching Indian-patterned blanket was a perfect color for the brown and white paint.

Cindy bent to pick it up. "This saddle weighs about a hundred pounds!" she said in surprise.

"Not really—just thirty." Max grinned. "Hook the stirrup over the saddle horn before you try to sling it," he advised.

With a grunt Cindy threw the saddle over Gold

Rush's back. "Doesn't it bother him that the saddle's so heavy?" she asked.

Max pointed at Gold Rush's huge shoulder muscles. "He's made for it. He's a cowboy horse—he could go all day under a Western saddle, and it's really comfortable to ride in. Riding Western isn't like racing, where you're trying to get the saddle's weight down so you can go fast."

Cindy cinched the saddle and adjusted the one-piece Western bridle on Gold Rush's head. She led the paint to the stable yard and mounted up.

Max followed with Dynamite, and within minutes they were riding across a large field. Cindy couldn't believe how good it felt to be on a horse again. She sat deep in the saddle, enjoying Gold Rush's rocking gait. The Western saddle was very comfortable, almost like sitting on a sofa.

"Gold Rush neck-reins," Max said, riding up beside her. "Instead of pulling his head around with a direct rein, just touch the side of his neck with the rein and he'll turn away from it."

Cindy tried it. "Wow, he's so sensitive!" she said as the big paint immediately veered off to the right in response to her touch with the left rein.

"Since he's a barrel racer, turning fast is his specialty," Max said.

"I'd like to try barrel racing," Cindy said.

"Run Gold Rush in a couple of figure eights to warm him up first. Then you could take him around that tree," Max suggested, pointing at a large oak in the middle of the field.

"Okay." Cindy squeezed with her legs, and Gold Rush immediately picked up a lope. The horse did effortless flying lead changes at the center of the eight. Then Cindy leaned back in the saddle, signaling Gold Rush to stop. The paint skidded to a halt so fast, Cindy almost slid off over his head.

"That's another specialty of Western horses—stopping on a dime," Max said, laughing.

"Now you tell me." Cindy pointed Gold Rush at the tree.

"Should I time you?" Max joked.

"No." Cindy felt a moment's uncertainty. She wasn't too sure of her seat in a Western saddle, and neck reining wasn't instinctive to her yet. But this was going to be fun, she decided. She cued Gold Rush forward.

The next instant the paint was flying at the tree. Cindy touched his neck with the rein and hung on to the saddle horn as Gold Rush leaned around the tree. The ground rushed up to meet them. Cindy felt the tops of the goldenrod underfoot brush her boot.

He's taken the turn too sharply—he's going to fall! she thought, but there was no time to steady the paint. At the last second Gold Rush dug into the ground and righted himself. With a burst of speed the paint charged back toward Max and Dynamite.

"That was great!" Cindy called, grinning as she reined Gold Rush in. She'd been scared, but the ride had been a thrill, too.

"We can trade horses if you want," Max said. "I like riding Gold Rush, too."

Cindy hesitated. She had to admit that riding Western was more exciting than she'd thought it would be. But she was longing to be back on a Thoroughbred. Besides, it would be fun to try out Max's horse.

"Let's switch," she said, dismounting and trading reins with Max. Cindy had to let down the stirrup to get on Dynamite—the Thoroughbred was at least sixteen hands tall, and the English stirrups were shorter than the Western ones.

The hot-blooded horse danced underneath her as she mounted up. Cindy easily restrained Dynamite with the reins. She could tell in a second that she was on a Thoroughbred. Riding the Quarter Horse had been great, but this would be heaven!

"Do you want to try a slow gallop?" Max asked, already wheeling Gold Rush.

"Yes!" Cindy followed him at an easy gallop. Dynamite's long, slender legs effortlessly ate up the ground between them. Max spurred Gold Rush, and the Quarter Horse leaped ahead.

"Hey, this isn't quite a slow gallop!" Cindy called.

"Didn't I tell you Gold Rush used to be a racehorse?" Max yelled back. "He used to run on the Quarter-Horse tracks." Max let Gold Rush out even more. But Dynamite was hot on their heels—he wasn't about to be left in the dust!

Cindy laughed from sheer exuberance as the two horses thundered across the field. *This is so perfect!* she thought. The hot summer wind buffeted her face as Dynamite eagerly pulled on the reins. She was impressed that Max had such a spirited horse.

"Want to race?" Max called.

"Maybe next time, when Dynamite and I know each other better," Cindy called back. *I'd really rather ride Gold Rush in a race*, she thought. *I'd like to see what that kind of speed is like.* She knew that Quarter Horses could run faster even than Thoroughbreds in races of up to a quarter mile. That was how Quarter Horses had gotten their name.

"Let me show you something!" Max pulled up Gold Rush on top of a small hill and gazed out over a green meadow dotted with goldenrod. "It's so great out here," he said.

"Does your mom own all this?" Cindy asked, stopping Dynamite beside him.

"Only fifty acres—but our neighbors don't mind if we ride on their land."

Cindy balanced one hand back on the cantle of the saddle and relaxed. The sun was a brilliant hot yellow circle in a bright blue sky. Cindy breathed in the sweet scent of clover and bluegrass and the heavier scent of ripening raspberries. "Don't you wish summer would never end?" she asked.

"Yeah, I think that every summer." Max nodded. "I wish school didn't start in a month."

Cindy smiled in agreement, enjoying the warm caress of the summer wind.

Max looked over at Cindy. "You said you'd tell me how Glory lost the Jim Dandy," he said. "I read in the newspaper that he was closing fast but came up short at the wire."

"He didn't really lose the race—the jockey did."

Cindy caught Max up on all the problems they'd had since Ashleigh had stopped riding the colt. "So we're stuck," she finished. "Ashleigh can't ride because she's pregnant, and Glory won't go well for anyone else."

"That's a problem." Max frowned in thought. "If you could ride him, I bet he'd be okay," he said.

"That's the only way I can see out of this, too—but it's impossible." Cindy sighed. "I have to be sixteen to ride Glory on the track. I've tried to think of some way I could ride him, but I haven't had any luck."

7

That afternoon Samantha dropped Cindy off at the big mall in Lexington where Cindy had arranged to meet Heather and Mandy.

"Cindy—over here!" Mandy was waving exuberantly at her from across the broad aisle, which was crowded with shoppers. Heather was right behind her.

Cindy ran to meet them, almost dropping the big folder she was carrying. Her friends had asked to see all the newspaper clippings about her and Glory. The press had made a big deal out of Cindy and Glory's rags-to-riches story, from Cindy's finding him as a frightened and abused animal to his astonishing victories at the track.

"Hey, your hair's longer!" Heather said excitedly. "Are you having fun living at Saratoga?"

"Yeah, but it's nice to be back." Cindy thought her friends looked a little different, too. Heather's skin, normally so pale, glowed with a light rosy tan.

Mandy was taller, and despite her braces, she looked in great physical shape. "I missed you guys!" Cindy added.

"So let's see those articles," Heather said, gesturing at Cindy's folder.

"Let's look at the articles after we shop, while we eat or something," Mandy suggested. "My mom will pick us up at four."

"I want to buy something for Ashleigh and Mike's baby, then go home," Cindy said firmly. Shopping definitely wasn't her favorite activity.

"It's amazing news that Ashleigh's pregnant," Heather said as they entered the department store.

"Yeah, isn't it? She doesn't really look any different yet, but she's really happy." *Even if Glory isn't,* Cindy added to herself.

"We should look for school clothes, too, since school starts soon," Heather said.

"I guess." Cindy glanced around the store.

"There's baby stuff," Mandy said, pointing to an aisle stocked with brightly colored plastic toys and racks of small outfits.

"Does Ashleigh know if it's a boy or a girl?" Heather asked.

"Not yet." Cindy examined a pair of booties. "I guess we don't know whether to buy things in pink or blue," she added.

"A lot of these clothes are yellow or green," Heather said as she leafed through a rack of tiny shorts outfits. Cindy walked around to the other side of the rack.

"Look at this tie-dyed sleeper!" Mandy exclaimed, holding it up. The tiny pajama with feet was colored with wild swirls of red, purple, and blue.

"I think she'd like that." Cindy took the sleeper and held it up to admire.

"You're already calling the baby a she," Heather pointed out.

"I am? Yeah, I guess that's what I want Ashleigh to have." Cindy wondered if the baby would be a rider when she grew up. If she was anything like her parents, she would be.

"Are we going to look for school clothes?" Mandy asked as they paid for the present at the register.

"I'm tired of shopping," Cindy said. "How much longer till your mom picks us up, Mandy?"

"Another hour."

"That leaves us just enough time to—" Cindy looked at her two friends and grinned.

"Go to the tack store!" Heather finished.

In the large, brightly lit tack store, Cindy headed straight for the saddles. Someday, when Glory's racing career was over, she wanted to have a beautiful saddle of her own to pleasure-ride him with. If she started saving now, she might have enough money in a few years to buy the saddle she'd been admiring.

On the way to the saddles Cindy passed the riding clothes section. *This is more like it!* she thought. "Hey, come here, you guys," she called. "I found our school clothes!"

"Where?" Heather and Mandy looked around the aisle.

"Look at these riding jeans." Cindy picked up a pair of hunter green jeans with knee patches on the inside of the legs.

"Riding clothes are the coolest!" Mandy said.

"Yeah," Heather agreed. "I can see us going to school in those jeans!"

"Me, too. Hey, there's Melissa and Laura." Cindy pointed. The two girls from Cindy and Heather's sixth-grade class had been examining bridles up the aisle. At the sound of Cindy's voice they looked up and sauntered over.

"Hi, you guys," Melissa said. She was a popular, wealthy girl. Cindy introduced her and Melissa's best friend, Laura, to Mandy. Cindy realized that she knew a lot more kids now than she had a year earlier. That was mostly because of Glory. A lot of the kids at school were knowledgeable about horses, and they had taken an interest in Glory's racing career.

"How's your summer going?" Cindy asked the other girls.

"Pretty good," Melissa said. "My dad's running a string at Arlington." Cindy knew that Melissa's father owned a large breeding and training stable near Lexington.

"We're riding a lot," Laura said. "Mostly exercise riding for Melissa's dad."

"Sounds fun." Cindy felt a little envious. She'd be lucky if she got in more than a day or two of riding for the rest of the summer. In just two days she would leave for the Saratoga track again.

"So how's Glory?" Melissa asked, sounding

envious, too. Cindy knew that despite Glory's recent defeat, he was still considered a star in racing.

"He's fine. We're prepping him for the Travers," she said.

"That's incredible." Melissa looked impressed. "We almost entered one of our horses in the Travers, but my father decided the competition was too stiff. And our horse was a champion at two."

Cindy knew the Travers was a difficult race. The other horses running would be some of the best in the world, and at a mile and a quarter it would be the longest race Glory had run yet. Glory would need to be at the top of his game to win it. *I really should be back at Saratoga, doing whatever I can to get him ready for the race,* Cindy thought. Suddenly she lost her taste for shopping, even in a tack store. "Isn't it time to go?" she asked.

"Yeah, my lesson starts in half an hour," Heather said.

"See you guys." Melissa and Laura waved.

Cindy and her friends found the Jarvises' car in the mall parking lot. "Well, how was it—did you shop till you dropped?" Mrs. Jarvis joked.

"Yeah. But we found a good present for Ashleigh's baby." Cindy patted her shopping bag. Going to the mall had been a chore, but the result was worth it, she thought.

At the Nelsons' stable Tor had just finished a lesson and was moving several large jumps into a corner. The ring seemed refreshingly cool and dim after the hot summer sunshine outside. "Ready to jump?" Tor asked Heather with a smile.

"Sure," Heather said shyly. "I'll have Sasha ready in just a minute." Sasha was one of Tor's gentle, well-trained jumpers. Tor used the bay mare to teach several beginning riders.

"Are you going to ride?" Cindy asked Mandy as she and the other girl settled into the bleachers at the side of the ring to watch Heather.

Mandy shook her head. "I already had a lesson early this morning. I'm getting ready for a show in Virginia next month. Did you know I'm riding against kids who aren't disabled? I did in my last show, too."

"And of course you won." Cindy was impressed.

Mandy laughed. "Of course!"

"Here comes Heather." Heather was sitting up straight on Sasha, with her hands just in front of the horse's withers and her heels down. She looked calm and in control. "She looks really good—a lot better than she did a couple of months ago," Cindy added.

"Yeah, she doesn't seem scared of the horse anymore."

Mandy's never been scared of anything, Cindy thought admiringly. "How are your blisters?" she asked. The gutsy little girl had kept riding the past spring even when her braces were rubbing quarter-size blisters on her legs.

"They're gone." Mandy loosened one of her braces and pulled up the leg of her riding breeches. "I don't get them anymore now that I've been putting in extra padding—see? I guess I'll have some scars, though."

"At least you're not in pain anymore," Cindy said

with relief. "So that's why you can compete at a higher level."

"Yeah, kind of." Mandy looked out intently at Heather and Sasha. "My legs still hurt a lot when I ride. I mean, they hurt all the time—the doctor says they're supposed to, because that means the braces are working to straighten them. They healed crookedly after the car accident."

"You get them off pretty soon, right?" Cindy said gently.

"Sometime next year." Mandy grinned. "I can't wait!"

Heather had finished her warm-up at a walk, posting trot, and canter. Tor had set up an easy, low jump course for her: a crossbar, two parallels, and a combination crossbar and parallel.

"Now I want you to get off Sasha and walk the course," Tor said to Heather. "Try to estimate how many strides she should take between each jump. With the jumps this low, you can probably get away with a poor takeoff point—the horse is a strong enough jumper to compensate. But as the jumps get higher, you won't have that luxury."

Cindy watched Heather carefully pace off the course. "Okay," she said. "I'm ready—if I can just remember everything!"

Tor nodded. "Give it a try."

Heather remounted and gathered her reins. With a frown of concentration she circled the mare at a trot, then a canter, and set her at the first crossbar.

"She's looking good," Mandy murmured as

Heather smoothly cantered the mare over the crossbar and two parallels. "But that combination coming up is a little tricky. If she misses the takeoff for the crossbar, it'll mess up her approach for the parallel. . . ."

"Oh, no!" Cindy gasped. Even though she had little experience jumping, she could see that Sasha had taken off much too soon for the combination. The mare landed jarringly far past the crossbar and almost on top of the parallel. Heather was unbalanced from the rocky landing and unable to give Sasha guidance, and so on her own the mare did a huge jump over the oncoming parallel. Heather almost fell off backward. Gripping Sasha's mane desperately, Heather barely kept her seat. She managed to stop the mare at the far end of the ring.

Tor walked over to them. "You got left," he said to Heather. "That's—"

"You don't need to tell me," Heather interrupted. She grimaced and rubbed her tailbone. "I got thrown back."

"The jump took you by surprise," Tor explained. "You needed to start planning your approach while you were in the air over the last jump."

"While I'm in the air!" Heather's eyes were wide. "I was just trying to hang on."

Tor laughed. "Well, hanging on is important, but if you'd planned for the jump correctly, you might not have been hanging on for dear life! Then you'd have gone with the horse instead of behind her. Try that combination again."

"Tor didn't say it, but getting left is a bad fault,"

Mandy said softly to Cindy. "You don't have control, and a lot of times leaning back like that punishes the horse's mouth."

Cindy nodded and smiled sympathetically at Heather as she and Sasha rounded the corner in front of them. She hoped Heather would get it right this time.

Heather did much better on the second round. "There's so much to remember," she complained as she trotted up to Tor, pushing back her light blond hair. "I'm trying to keep my legs and hands in the right position *and* watch exactly how to take the jumps. But we're going so fast!"

"You should try steeplechasing," Tor said with a laugh. "You're racing, with all the dangers of moving on a horse at speed, and you're also jumping in a pack of horses. If one goes down, sometimes the rest fall like dominoes. Speaking of which—" Tor glanced at his watch. "I was going to exercise Sierra for a while. His 'chase at Saratoga is in just over a week, and I want to keep him up to form. Let's put up Sasha and go over to Whitebrook."

Heather efficiently brushed Sasha in her stall and wiped down her tack, then the girls climbed in Tor's car. On the drive over to Whitebrook, Heather and Mandy caught Cindy up on all the news about the kids at school. Cindy was surprised at how much she'd missed. She realized she had been gone a long time.

At the stable Len had Sierra up in a stall, waiting for Tor. Tor quickly saddled the big horse and headed him out to the inner turf course—before Sierra had time to think up any tricks, Cindy assumed.

"Did I tell you what he did this morning?" Cindy asked her friends as they walked out to the course, crossing the dirt track.

"Nope," Mandy said. "Did he run away?"

"Got it in one." Cindy related Sierra's morning escapade over the paddock fence.

"Sierra's such a pill." Heather shook her head.

"But boy, can he jump," Mandy said with admiration.

The three friends sat in the grass at the edge of the turf course. Cindy looked out to the course. Tor had completed Sierra's warm-ups and was pointing him toward a four-foot brush jump. The big liver chestnut wasn't playing around now. His ears were pricked with interest as he pounded across the deep green course, lifted over the brush jump, gathered his legs beneath him, and galloped on.

Cindy sighed happily, running her hands through the thick, cool grass. As she watched the magnificent horse and his rider take jump after jump, Cindy felt as if she could soar into the clear blue sky with them.

8

"I'm not sure I really want Beth to come back," Cindy confessed the next morning to Samantha as they washed the breakfast dishes in the kitchen. Samantha and Cindy had just finished a big breakfast of waffles with Vermont maple syrup, freshly squeezed orange juice, and milk for Cindy, coffee for Samantha.

"Why not?" Samantha raised a quizzical eyebrow. "You and Beth usually get along fine."

"It's not that—I'm just used to no bedtimes or mealtimes." Cindy toweled off the last dish and carefully placed it in the rack.

Samantha laughed. "Cindy, you're so responsible, you don't *need* anyone telling you to go to bed or eat. But when Beth gets here tonight, don't tell her I've been letting you run wild." Beth was scheduled to fly into Lexington that night to check on her aerobics business. The next day Samantha would fly back to Saratoga to help get Shining ready for the Whitney, and Cindy, Mike, and Beth would drive back up to the track with Sierra and Clover.

"I only told Mom and Dad good stuff about what we've been doing." Cindy had talked with her parents just the night before.

"Glory's as happy as a clam," Ian had said when Cindy had anxiously asked about the colt. "But I'm a wreck trying to figure out what to do with him next, and so is Mike. We've been waiting to see how he came out of the race, but soon we'll have to put him back on the track." Cindy had heard in her father's voice that he was afraid the trouble would start again then.

"What are your plans for today?" Samantha asked, interrupting Cindy's thoughts.

"I wanted to spend some time with Four Leaf Clover." Cindy hung the dishtowel on the refrigerator door. "I thought I'd brush him down really well and walk him to keep him fit for the auction."

Samantha finished mopping off the counter. "Good idea. Ashleigh and I are going to shop for maternity clothes for her."

"When do you think I should give Ashleigh and Mike the baby's present?" Cindy asked. She had already shown Samantha the tiny sleeper she'd bought at the mall.

"Well, at some point we'll have a baby shower for her," Samantha answered. "But you might give it to her at a special moment instead. I know she's been feeling down lately. She can't ride, and she can't even train because she's stuck here until she and the

Townsends reach an agreement about Wonder's Champion. They're giving her a really hard time."

"What do they want?" Cindy felt nervous.

"They're saying that the only way they'll accept Wonder's Champion being trained here is if all Wonder's other offspring go to Townsend Acres. Ashleigh just can't do that, Cindy. You know that Princess and Mr. Wonderful are injured, and even Pride had a close call with his life once. He needs special care, too."

"They have to stay here," Cindy agreed.

Samantha sighed. "So I don't know how Ashleigh and the Townsends will resolve it. When Ashleigh got a half interest in Wonder, that was the best thing that ever happened to her—and in some ways the worst. At least that's what I think. Ashleigh's had a say in the training and care of Wonder and all her offspring, but at every step of the way she's had to deal with so much aggravation from the Townsends."

Cindy just nodded. She had no idea how Ashleigh would sort it out about Wonder's Champion.

When Cindy stepped out the door, she saw Clover grazing in the front paddock with the five other yearlings at the farm. The chestnut colt's head jerked up.

"Here, boy!" she called.

The next moment all the yearlings were running for the gate. Rainbow and Clover were in the lead, nipping and chasing each other. The twin yearlings loved people. They'd been spoiled by Cindy, Len, and Vic since they were born.

"Ready for a walk?" Cindy asked as she slipped a halter on Clover. "We'd better go now, before it gets any hotter."

The summer day was already humid and very warm. Cindy led the colt toward the big trees along the lane.

"See you later!" Samantha called from the drive.

"Okay!" Cindy waved at her and Ashleigh, who was just climbing into her car.

Cindy looked back at Clover. The young horse was following obediently, swishing his tail at flies. "It still seems so weird that Ashleigh can't ride," she said to him. "I wish she'd get things straightened out here so that she could at least come up to Saratoga to train."

Clover flicked his ears, listening. He had always been so responsive to people. Cindy hoped he would go to a loving home, not one where he was just expected to run. Cindy had often tried to tell herself that horses weren't as sensitive as people about things like that, but she didn't really believe it.

Cindy mentally shook herself. She had a job to do with the colt. "Let's trot!" she told him. Clover instantly responded, lightly moving after her on a loose lead.

Cindy kept going until they reached the edge of Whitebrook's property. They'd come over a mile, she realized as she mopped her damp blond hair off her forehead. Bees droned heavily in the flowery fields, and a magnificent pile of thunderclouds in hues of blue and gray was building to the west. The day was so peaceful, she thought.

"You're great company," she said to Clover, rubbing the diamond on his forehead. "Just like Glory." *Except after you leave here, you won't ever come back again,* she thought sadly.

The colt leaned happily into her caresses, and Cindy pushed away her unhappy thoughts. She knew she had to enjoy what little time she had left with the colt.

The next morning Cindy was anxious to leave for Saratoga. Late the following night she'd be reunited with Glory, and the next day Shining would run in the Whitney. Cindy wanted to help Samantha prepare the filly with brushings, exercise, and a lot of love.

Cindy had already checked the storage compartment of the trailer to make sure they had brought all the veterinary supplies, feed, and tack that Sierra and Clover would need. Then she'd stowed the suitcases in the truck.

Beth had arrived from the airport the night before, and Samantha had flown out to Saratoga. "The changing of the guard," Beth had joked.

Cindy had smiled, but within minutes she *felt* guarded. It was good to see Beth again, but right away she'd insisted on preparing a big dinner. Cindy had wanted to spend the time she had left with the horses, especially Clover.

"Dinner won't take long, Cindy," Beth had said, as if she'd read her mind. "And as an athlete, you should know that if you eat a good meal, you'll have more energy for whatever you do."

Cindy had known Beth was right, but she hadn't wanted to spend much time on dinner anyway.

Mike and Tor were carefully loading Four Leaf Clover into one of the stalls of the two-horse trailer while Ashleigh looked on. Cindy walked quickly over and put a steadying hand on the colt's side. "That's a boy," she encouraged. Clover stepped into the trailer and took a bite of hay from his net.

"We just have to load Sierra—then we're ready to go," Mike said.

"Your fifth passenger," Ashleigh joked as Tor led Sierra out of the training barn.

Cindy realized immediately that she hadn't counted on the big chestnut's willfulness when she'd reckoned they'd get out of town soon. In dismay and growing impatience, Cindy watched as Sierra danced at the end of the lead rope Mike was holding, veering off first to one side of the trailer, then the other. In fact, he was going everywhere but inside it, Cindy thought.

"Sierra, I've about had it with you," Tor said in exasperation as Sierra backed up, shaking his head vigorously. Tor was standing behind Sierra, trying to push him in, but the big horse was pushing Tor harder in the other direction. "What is your problem? I shouldn't have to baby you to get you to load."

"Speaking of babying Sierra—have you been feeding him in the trailer, Ash?" Mike asked.

"I was, but he loaded perfectly for his last 'chase. I quit because I thought he'd finally mended his ways," Ashleigh said ruefully. "Guess not, huh?"

Sierra lightly pawed the ground with a front hoof, his intelligent dark eyes fixed on Tor. If Cindy hadn't been in such a hurry and worried that Sierra might get hurt in the struggle, she would have laughed at the stallion's expression. He seemed to be saying, *Giving up so soon?*

"We can pull the trailer up to one of the fences— then he can't duck out on that side," Mike said. "And get a longer rope so that we have more play in it. I don't want to let go and have to chase him."

"Try putting some sweet feed in the trailer," Ashleigh suggested.

"I'll get it," Cindy said, hurrying to the barn. She knew Sierra loved the sticky, molasses-coated grain.

When she got back with a bucket, Sierra was looking at the new position of the trailer near the fence, the long rope, and the determined expressions of the two men. He stretched his long neck toward Cindy and sniffed. Then he whinnied.

"Come on, Sierra," Cindy coaxed, pouring the sweet feed in the front box of the trailer as noisily as possible.

"Sierra, you pest," Tor said, pulling on the rope.

Sierra watched Cindy and the bucket for a moment. Then he walked calmly into the trailer, as if to say, *Now that I've shown you who's boss, I'll be glad to go in.*

"He wasted an hour of our time." Mike sighed. "We've got to push off. Bye, Ash," he said, and kissed Ashleigh affectionately. "I hope you get the situation with the Townsends cleared up so we can see you really soon."

"I'll do my best." Ashleigh frowned. "But this is a tough one."

"See you Wednesday, Sammy," Tor said. Cindy knew that Tor would meet them at Saratoga the day before Sierra's steeplechase. Until then he had his hands full at his own stable.

"Ready, everyone?" Mike asked.

"I am." Cindy hopped in the truck, thanking her lucky stars that Sierra could be bribed with sweet feed. Through the trailer window she saw that the big horse's nose was buried in the treat. Cindy only wished the problem with Glory could be solved so easily.

Maybe it can be, she thought, stretching out her legs across the backseat of the truck to get comfortable. *I'll bet there's something we overlooked that will work.*

"Glory, I'm here!" Cindy called the next night, running down the barn aisle to Glory's stall. The drive up had been grueling, but seeing Glory's elegant gray head poked out of the stall, an eager expression in his dark eyes, made her forget completely how tired she was. Beth had tried to convince Cindy to stop at the B&B first and rest a while, but Cindy wouldn't hear of it.

Glory whinnied throatily, bobbing his head. Cindy threw her arms around his neck. "Oh, boy, I missed you so much. But I'm back for good now," she reassured him. "For three weeks, anyway." Cindy felt a small trickle of cold run down her back as she remembered that school would start then, but she pushed away the thought. For the moment she and Glory were together, and that was all that mattered.

Cindy let herself into the stall and closely examined her horse. In the dim light Glory gleamed a soft, mysterious silver. "You look like a magic horse," she told him, dropping a kiss on his nose. "I just hope the magic comes back to your running."

Glory snorted and backed away, as if he were insulted that she doubted him for a moment.

"Cindy!" Ian grabbed her in a big hug. Cindy hugged her dad back and looked behind him. Samantha was hurrying toward her, followed by Len. No wonder Glory had jumped back at the sight of them all, Cindy thought with a grin. She was so glad to see everybody.

"Is Shining all set for tomorrow?" she asked Samantha, moving to the roan filly's stall. Shining was standing calmly, flicking an ear with interest at their conversation. In the dim light her sleek red and white coat was a deep maroon, blending into the black of her mane and tail.

"Couldn't be better," Samantha assured her. "She put in a fantastic work four days ago."

"What about Glory?" Cindy asked hopefully. "Did he go well with any jockey?"

"No, not yet," Ian said soberly. "We just have to hope that he'll run for one of them soon."

The next afternoon, the day of the Whitney, Cindy, and Len led Shining to the saddling paddock to join Shining's new jockey. The big old trees cast patches of cool, refreshing shadow. Cindy admired the dappling of deeper red on Shining's glossy coat as they passed in and out of the shade.

"I'm optimistic about this race," Len said as the spirited filly pranced behind Cindy, arching her neck. "Shining's works have been mighty fine."

"They sure have." Cindy smiled broadly. She couldn't agree more. Over the past two weeks Shining had put in very impressive clockings for Doug Tyler, the jockey who had replaced Ashleigh as Shining's rider. Glory hadn't.

Cindy's face fell slightly. Because Shining was going so well under Doug, Ian and Mike had immediately tried him out on Glory. That hadn't worked out nearly as well. The colt tended to lug in toward the rail when Doug rode him—not much, Cindy observed, because Doug was an excellent rider. He'd tried to compensate by pulling Glory's head around and waving the whip at his left side. But the colt hadn't given him a hundred percent.

Glory was different from Shining, Cindy thought as the filly affectionately lipped her shoulder. Shining and Glory had both gone from being timid, abused horses to stars at the track. But Shining was much more willing than Glory—she was less likely to fight a rider or play around. *Glory really is hard to ride*, Cindy thought. *I guess it is pretty amazing that he minds me!*

Samantha and Ian were waiting in the saddling paddock. "Hey, girl," Samantha said softly as Shining approached. The filly strained eagerly toward Samantha, looking for caresses from her owner.

Cindy smiled. Samantha and Shining loved each other just as much as she and Glory did.

"She's ready to give it her all today." Len handed Samantha Shining's reins and hoisted the small racing saddle onto the filly's back.

"I hope we didn't make a mistake entering her against colts," Samantha said, frowning as she checked the girth. "We could have run her in the Go for Wand or another of the big races for mares and fillies instead."

"I don't think Shining is overmatched." Ian smiled reassuringly at Samantha. "The race is only a mile and an eighth. I'd be more concerned at a mile and a quarter—but she won against colts at that distance in the Suburban."

"Laugh It Off is going off as the favorite, but Shining's the second favorite," Cindy said. Laugh It Off, a tall bay, was coming off impressive victories in the Midwest.

Doug Tyler walked over to join them. Cindy noticed that the short, wiry man was looking Shining over carefully as he listened to Ian. No jockey wanted to ride an unsound horse and risk the often tragic consequences of an accident on the track.

"Rate her through the early fractions if you can," Ian said to Doug. "She's got to have something left for the last eighth. Laugh It Off has a powerful closing kick, and so do Magnificent Seven and Honey's Ride."

Doug nodded. "Okay—if Shining will stand for it. She likes to be on the lead."

Len gave the jockey a leg into the saddle.

Samantha drew a deep breath. "Good luck, Doug," she said.

Doug gathered the reins and touched his whip to his helmet. "See you in the winner's circle."

"Beth and Mike are waiting for us at our seats," Ian said. "Shall we go find them?"

Samantha nodded mutely. Cindy wondered for a second why Samantha always got so nervous before Shining's races. The filly had a stunning record at the track. Then Cindy remembered how confident she had been before Glory's first stakes race—and how the colt had tested positive for drugs soon afterward and been disqualified. The outcome of a race was never certain, she supposed. Probably there were many other dangers and risks inherent in racing that she wasn't even aware of.

Beth waved at them from their seats in the grandstand. "Hurry," she called. "Here comes Shining."

Shining had just stepped onto the track for the post parade. The filly was crabstepping and throwing up her head. A slight sweat darkened her red and white coat. Cindy sat beside Beth and focused her binoculars.

"Shining's wired," Cindy commented. Then she wondered if she should have said that. It would only make Samantha more nervous, and she could see Shining's condition for herself. In the Metropolitan in May, Shining had used herself up before the race and lost by a neck. The filly had gotten so overexcited, Samantha had thought she was drugged as well as Glory.

"Shining's going to have to be wired to beat this field," Mike remarked, leaning around Beth.

"I bet Shining knows that," Cindy said. She knew from long association that the filly was extremely intelligent.

Samantha laughed. "Thanks, Cindy. You always know how to put the right slant on things."

The eight horses in the field entered the gate one at a time in their post order. Shining was the number-two horse. Laugh It Off, Magnificent Seven, and Honey's Ride were numbers three, four, and five, respectively.

"Shining has an excellent post position," Ian said approvingly.

The starting bell rang the instant the last horse was in the gate. Shining lunged out with enormous strides, cutting in front of the number-one horse toward the rail.

The people in front of Cindy jumped to their feet. "Run for it, Shining!" shouted one man.

Cindy peered between their shoulders, trying to see. Shining was on the lead! The roan filly had a three-length margin over her nearest contenders after a quarter mile. The horses settled in, maintaining their positions around the clubhouse turn.

"Shining's got it!" Cindy said excitedly. "No one's catching up to her!"

"Not yet." Ian's face was tense. "Some of the horses are being rated—they haven't been asked to give everything yet. Doug just tried to rate Shining, but she was getting rank on him. He had to let her out."

"Fast fractions set so far," commented the announcer. "And they're coming up on the three-quarter pole. Shining's losing ground!"

"Here come the closers!" Samantha cried.

Her heart in her throat, Cindy watched as Laugh It Off, Magnificent Seven, and Honey's Ride roared into the stretch. They narrowed Shining's lead to two lengths. Then they were right behind her.

Cindy couldn't believe the powerful closing kick the colts had. They had found another gear, almost as if they hadn't been racing until then.

"And Shining faces a three-horse challenge," the announcer called.

"Go, baby! Reach for it!" Samantha screamed.

Cindy could see that Shining was determined to fight it out. Magnificent Seven had drawn even with her flank to threaten. Doug kneaded his hands rapidly along Shining's neck, asking for more speed.

Shining responded! The filly began to draw clear at the eighth pole, slowly at first, then with increasing authority. Now Cindy could hear the muffled snorts of the horses and the heavy pounding of their hooves as they churned up the soft dirt, heading for home.

Flicking her tail in farewell to the colts, Shining coasted under the wire. The dueling colts flashed across the finish instants later, several lengths behind.

"And it's an astonishing victory for Shining against a furious late charge by the colts," the announcer cried. "What a filly! And she beat the boys in the Suburban just last month, folks."

"A three-way photo finish for second." Ian looked amazed. "That's certainly unusual."

"There's no doubt who's first!" Samantha had tears of joy in her eyes.

In the winner's circle Samantha, Mike, and Ian were hit with a barrage of congratulations and questions from the reporters. With a big smile and a thumbs-up, Doug jumped off Shining and went to weigh in with his saddle.

"Good girl!" Samantha hugged Shining and pressed her cheek to the filly's wet neck. "I'm so proud of you!"

"With this second victory over the colts, are you considering starting Shining in the Breeders' Cup Classic?" one of the reporters asked Samantha as they posed with Shining for the winner's photo.

"It's early days yet," Samantha responded. "But yes, that's been in the back of our minds."

Cindy looked at Samantha in surprise. Until that moment Samantha hadn't mentioned that Shining might be running in the Breeders' Cup Classic. Shining had been an almost sure starter in the Distaff, a race at a mile and one-eighth for fillies and mares on Breeders' Cup day. The Classic was a mile and a quarter, for fillies and colts age three and up.

"Come on, girl," Cindy said to Shining, collecting the reins from Doug. "Let's get you cooled out."

Cindy looked closely at Shining as she led the filly to the backside. Shining's victory had been glorious, but the race had taken a lot out of her. It wasn't just that her breathing was still harsh and fast. Cindy knew Shining so well. Just from the way the filly was walking, Cindy could tell the horse was exhausted. Shining was gingerly favoring all her legs, as if the muscles hurt in every one.

Cindy patted the tired horse's neck sympathetically. Shining rubbed her head hard against Cindy's shoulder. She seemed still wired from her effort.

Mentally Cindy compared Shining to Glory. So far, when Glory was drug-free, he came out of races well at any distance. But Shining had shown an incredible amount of heart that day.

I wonder who would win if Glory and Shining raced each other, Cindy thought. *Shining would give Glory a run for his money, that's for sure.*

9

"That's a perfect boy," Cindy praised as she led Four Leaf Clover around the stable yard at the auction grounds three days later. She wanted to exercise him a little to relax him and give him some fun. It would be the last they ever had together, Cindy thought, feeling her throat tighten. That night the colt would be auctioned at the Fasig-Tipton selected yearling sale, beginning at eight o'clock.

With a barely perceptible tug on the lead line, Cindy signaled the colt to halt. The elegant young Thoroughbred raised his head and sniffed the fresh breeze that had sprung up with the cool of evening. Two days earlier the August heat had broken, and a hint of fall was in the air. A leaf fluttered down from a nearby tree.

Cindy caught the leaf between her fingers and twirled it. The colt craned his neck around to nibble the leaf.

"Here you go," Cindy said, stroking his glossy neck. "You can have anything you want for the next few minutes, I promise."

Cindy had been reminding herself all day to act like a professional handler. The other handlers walking horses around the grounds looked businesslike and detached, and she should be the same way about Clover. After all, in an hour he wouldn't belong to Whitebrook anymore.

But as she looked at the gorgeous colt a wave of sadness washed over her. She hugged him as if she'd never let go. "We've been together so long," she said softly. "I don't want you to leave."

Clover watched her with his big dark eyes. Then he shook himself hard.

"You're right—I need to snap out of it," Cindy said with a sigh.

This is the way it has to be, she reminded herself as she led the colt back to his stall. She couldn't keep him out long, because prospective buyers might want to see him before the auction. *I'm starting school in a couple of weeks, and Clover is, too.* He would begin training soon and possibly race as a two-year-old the next spring or summer.

Cindy resolutely shut the door to the stall and turned away. She had gone only a few steps when Clover whinnied.

"I forgot your treat!" Cindy dug into her jeans pocket and found a small, tender carrot. Fighting tears, she walked back to the stall and held it out to the colt. Clover gently lipped it from her hand.

"Good-bye, sweetie," Cindy whispered, rubbing his satiny neck for the last time.

"Cindy?" Beth called from the end of the aisle. "It's about time for the auction."

"I don't want to go." Cindy tried to compose her face.

"You don't?" Beth asked in surprise. "Ian and Mike may bid on some horses."

"Yeah, I know." Cindy shook her head firmly. "But I'd rather just look around." Ordinarily she would have loved to go to the auction. Nothing was more exciting to her than watching her dad and Mike pick out fantastic horses to bid on and then bring the farm's newest prospects home. "You can tell me all about the auction afterward," Cindy added. She hoped they would all tell her that Clover had found a wonderful home. But she had no desire to see the beautiful colt sold.

Beth still looked surprised. Then sudden understanding dawned on her face. "Oh, I see," she said gently. "I'm sorry, Cindy. Why don't we just meet you back here in about two hours?"

"Okay." Cindy was glad when Beth left to join the others.

She walked around the auction grounds, looking at the young sale horses and trying to cheer herself up. Some of the horses were unsettled by the strange territory and the commotion. Cindy watched a well-muscled bay balk at an oddly shaped pile of straw, backing up and shaking his head. The groom coaxed the colt to walk around the straw, but the young horse was still nervously crabstepping.

I know Clover isn't frightened, Cindy comforted herself. He had learned to trust people from the day he was born. He would probably enjoy all the attention at the auction. She felt a little better thinking about the gorgeous colt prancing into the ring and the rippling murmur of appreciation from the audience.

Cindy sighed heavily. It would have helped her mood if Glory were behaving himself. But the previous day he'd put in another bad work for still another jockey. Cindy had lost track of who they were, there had been so many.

"Hey, Cindy!" Anne was standing right next to her. "I've been calling to you for about ten minutes. Can't you hear?"

"Hi," Cindy said, already trying to think how she could get away. *Anne's the last person I want to see now,* she thought. She didn't think the sassy California girl could possibly understand what she was going through.

Anne wore a short green riding vest against the slight chill of the evening and black English lace-up riding boots. Cindy yearned for a pair of those boots. But her parents were adamant that the boots were too expensive to wear for riding and around the stable.

Anne hardly seemed aware of her elegant attire. *She really looks at least sixteen,* Cindy thought enviously.

"What are you doing?" Anne asked.

Cindy shrugged. "Just walking around. What are you doing?"

"Kind of celebrating." Anne frowned. "Did you hear that our horse Sky Larking won the Nijana?"

110

"No, I didn't." Cindy had been too busy at Whitebrook, and then back at Saratoga helping to get Shining ready for the Whitney, to pay attention to that race.

Anne colored slightly. "Well, I know it's not like winning the Whitney!"

"That's really good news, though," Cindy said quickly. She hadn't meant to sound snobby.

"Yeah, I guess." Anne blew out a breath. "But it doesn't feel good to me."

"Why?" Cindy looked at the other girl in surprise. "Your dad must want his horses to win stakes races more than anything."

"Yeah, but they're not *his* horses. Sky Larking is already going to another trainer. A lot of times when the horses my dad trains start to do well, the owners just take them away and give them to more-famous trainers. My father keeps hoping he'll break through and get to keep training the best horses, but it hasn't happened yet."

"Well, maybe he'll get to soon," Cindy said.

Anne shrugged, then her shoulders slumped. "I guess I'm used to losing horses, since none of the horses my father trains are really ours."

Cindy could see that Anne wasn't used to it at all. Her heart went out to the other girl.

"There was one horse. . . ." Anne's dark eyes were dreamy. "He came to us when he was a yearling. I'd never seen a horse like him. He was a light bay, with the longest black mane and tail. My dad said he was perfect to train—smart, and he moved so fast and so gracefully, it was like he was Pegasus—you know, the winged horse?"

Cindy nodded.

"So that's what I called him. I took care of him, and we were really close. I used to hope a miracle would happen and he'd stay with us. It was so weird. I knew he'd go back to his owner at two to race, but I just couldn't deal with it when it happened. That was last summer."

"So how's he doing?" Cindy asked gently.

"I don't know. I never heard. I guess that means he never did much—if he'd won big races, I'd have seen him on TV."

Cindy realized that she couldn't feel sorry for herself about Clover when Anne had it so much worse. *I have my dream horse—Glory,* she thought. Wonder's Champion and the other Whitebrook horses were many more dreams to come.

"You're a lot braver than I am," Cindy said with a sigh. "I only lost one special horse today. But I don't feel great."

"What do you mean?" Anne looked curious.

Cindy explained about losing Clover at the auction. She hesitated for a moment, wondering if she should tell Anne why the colt had meant so much to her—that when she'd come to Whitebrook, she didn't have a friend in the world. Clover and his twin brother had been her first friends.

"Well, a horse like Clover has pretty good prospects," Anne said sympathetically when Cindy finished the story.

"I know. I don't really have anything to complain about." *But I still wish I looked like you*, Cindy thought, looking at Anne's polished boots.

"What are you staring at?" Anne demanded.

Cindy laughed. Maybe she'd better tell Anne how she felt about her clothes and attitude. Anne seemed to love horses, too—she wasn't so bad after all. "I'm staring at your boots," she said. "I want to steal them. That's the only way I'll ever get a pair. You always look so cool."

"You think *I'm* cool? Do you know what I've heard about you and horses?" Anne asked in astonishment. "You get to exercise-ride March to Glory, one of the best racehorses in the world. You're the groom for Shining, the filly who can beat the colts. You're from Whitebrook, home of Kentucky Derby and Classic winners. How do you think I feel when I'm around someone like you?"

Cindy grinned. "Not so cool?"

"That's right."

"Look, my dad started out years ago training claimers in Florida," Cindy said. "He got his first break with a horse named Gulfstream Waves. Gulfstream went on to become a stakes winner. So we haven't always been famous."

"My dad is hoping Sky Larking's win in the Nijana will be his big break." Anne frowned. After a few moments she said, "I'm sorry if I've acted grouchy or stuck-up. It's just that a couple of the well-known trainers and owners here have really been jerks to my mom and dad."

"Sorry," Cindy said. She guessed she could see Anne's point.

"Well, it's not your fault." Anne smiled reluctantly.

"I think we've both got a lot going for us," Cindy said firmly. "Truce?"

Anne smiled back. "Truce."

"Do you want to walk around and look at the horses?" Cindy asked. "That's what I was doing."

"How about sometime soon? I have to meet my parents in a minute," Anne said.

"Sounds good." Cindy waved good-bye.

She walked to one of the barns to check out a magnificent black filly that a groom had just led inside. *Now that Anne and I are getting along, I'll have a friend to share the rest of the Saratoga meet with*, Cindy thought.

She entered the barn, squinting as she tried to see in the dim light. The filly was in crossties at the end of the barn, lightly stamping her hoof.

A man was bent over to examine the hoof. *He seems so familiar*, Cindy thought. The man straightened and carefully set down the horse's hoof as she approached.

"Ben!" Cindy could barely take it in that he was there. She'd hoped so much to find Glory's first trainer, and suddenly he was right in front of her.

"Hello, Cindy." Ben smiled warmly. "It's good to see you. How have you been?"

"Fine—how are you?" Cindy forced herself to remember her manners. She couldn't immediately start telling him all about Glory's problems.

"I've been well. And so have the horses." Ben

stroked the glossy neck of the filly. The beautiful animal bobbed her head impatiently, tugging at the crossties.

"I've been looking for you," Cindy blurted.

"Well, here I am. And I'll be here for the rest of the meet." Ben unclipped the filly's leads. "Just let me put this girl away, then we can talk."

"She's one of yours?" Cindy asked, admiring the filly's satiny black coat, rippling over her shoulder and hindquarter muscles.

"This is Sucha Doll. She's going to auction tomorrow night." Ben scratched the filly's ears affectionately.

"I hope she sells for a lot," Cindy said politely.

"She should. She's out of a Secretariat mare and in general has superb breeding," Ben said as he shut the stall door on the filly. "And how is our silver star, March to Glory, doing?" Ben turned to look at Cindy keenly.

"I guess you didn't get my letter. I wrote you to tell you we're having trouble with him." Cindy quickly explained how poorly Glory had been going under every jockey except Ashleigh. "And Ashleigh can't ride anymore, because she's pregnant," she finished. "No one knows what to do."

"Ah, that's why Ashleigh stopped riding," Ben said. "I thought she must be injured. Well, it's good news that she's going to have a baby."

"Yes, except for Glory," Cindy blurted.

"I did see Glory lose the Jim Dandy on simulcast." Ben frowned. "What do you think happened?"

"He just didn't settle," Cindy said, her voice filled with frustration. "I think he got his signals from the jockey confused, and then he ran out of time at the end of the race."

"The descriptions of his performance in the racing papers weren't flattering," Ben remarked. "I'm sure everyone at Whitebrook was very disappointed."

"We were," Cindy confessed. "But I wasn't that surprised when he lost. Glory has always been so hard to handle. I mean, except for me and Ashleigh."

"Well, you have to humor the great horses," Ben remarked. "I knew one filly that couldn't stand crowds. She had a curtain over her stall door so that no one could bother her in between races, and she had to be rushed through the walking ring so that all the people watching didn't make her crazy. But then she'd get out on the track and run away with the prize. Glory's the finest—he's good enough to merit special treatment, too."

"But we don't know what that treatment should be," Cindy said desperately. She had been hoping for weeks that Ben would know what to do about Glory, but he didn't seem to. "I know if I could ride him, it would help. But there's no way my parents would let me break the track rules." Cindy again wished fervently that she were older.

For a second Cindy considered sneaking Glory out onto the track, either very early in the morning or late at night. Then she could ride him in secret. That had worked brilliantly the last time she had done it, on Whitebrook's track, right after she'd found Glory wandering in the woods. *I got Glory conditioned, and everyone saw what a great racehorse he is,* she thought.

Cindy shook her head. The plan had worked, but she knew it had been only by sheer luck. She'd almost gotten killed when Glory had gone out of control, *and* she'd been in major trouble with her dad for galloping a horse without permission.

Ben looked thoughtful for a moment. "I agree with you that Glory would probably go better if he were ridden occasionally by someone who knows how to handle him," he said. "Since you can't ride on the track, we'll have to think of something else."

"What?" Cindy asked eagerly. She couldn't believe it—Ben agreed that she should ride!

The trainer smiled broadly. "Actually, I already had in mind a little excursion for you and me here at Saratoga. We'll change the plan a bit and invite Glory along. It will be just the place for you to take a ride."

"Where?" Cindy was dying of curiosity. "And when?"

"Slow down!" Ben laughed. "I have to talk to your parents about this first. We'll go soon if they give their permission. And I won't tell you where we're going. It'll be more fun if it's a surprise."

Cindy didn't really think so, but she wasn't complaining. All that mattered was that she was going to get to ride Glory. She was sure her parents would let her, as long as it was safe.

"I'd better go meet my family," she said.

"I'd like to see Ian and Beth again. How about if

we all have dinner tonight?" Ben asked. "I'll call your parents later and find out if tonight is convenient."

"Great!" Cindy gave him the name and number of the B&B. Maybe at dinner she could get it out of Ben where they were going.

Cindy wandered around the backside, looking for Samantha or their dad and admiring the exquisite horses. A lot of them still wore their hip numbers from the auction and were probably with their new owners. Cindy felt better, even though she knew from the program that Clover's turn must have come and gone by now. She wondered with fresh curiosity what horse, if any, her dad and Mike had bought at the auction.

"Cindy, guess what?" Samantha was hurrying toward her through the crowds, a huge smile on her face. "Clover sold for an incredible price. It was the third-highest price for a colt in the whole sale!"

"And he was sold to Byerly Stables," Ian said, coming up behind Samantha.

Cindy thought for a moment. "Where's that?" she asked. She had heard of most of the major racing stables in Kentucky. Byerly must be out of state.

"Brace yourself," Samantha said excitedly. "It's in Arabia!"

"It is?" Cindy was stunned. Clover was going halfway around the world! This really was good-bye.

"For a long time Byerly Stables has been a major presence at Thoroughbred sales in this country," Ian said. "They've been wintering their horses in Arabia and racing them in Europe. It's possible that when

Clover is of racing age, he'll run at the new sand track at Nad al Sheba in Dubai."

"The Dubai World Cup will be held there next year. It's a new race featuring the best horses from the Americas, Europe, Arabia, and Oceania," Mike added.

In her sudden grief Cindy could hardly understand what they were talking about. "I wonder if they'll still call him Clover," she said. Her voice quivered.

"He'll have the best possible training and care at a wealthy farm like that," Beth said, putting her arm around Cindy's shoulders. "Who knows? Maybe we'll go see him run in Arabia someday."

Cindy nodded, but she still felt like crying.

"Guess what?" Ian said encouragingly. "We bought a horse at the auction. Here he comes with Mike."

Cindy looked around Ian and Beth. Mike was leading a tall, elegant gray yearling with a quick, graceful way of going. The horse was a solider gray than Glory, with a silvery gray mane and tail. Cindy could see that although the horse was frightened by the strange surroundings and handler, he was trying to be a gentleman about it and mind.

Cindy's heart went out to him. The colt might be big, but he was hardly more than a baby.

"Meet Storm's Ransom," Mike said. "We got him for an excellent price."

"He was way undervalued." Ian ran a hand over the horse's glossy gray neck. "His sire, Excellent

Prize, was a decent sprinter but has produced very few winners, and his dam, Rudy's Ruby, is an unraced daughter of Taken by Storm. But I like the cross of this colt. Taken by Storm was a champion sprinter and won several grade-one races before he was sidelined with an injury. In the past Rudy's Ruby was bred to stayers—horses who went the distance. Her foals never did much at the track."

"Previous breeders hoped that with Ruby's sprinter bloodlines, she'd produce a superhorse that could handle any distance," Samantha said. "The breeding to Excellent Prize is the first to a sprinter and may result in an excellent runner."

"I'm ready to take a chance on Storm's Ransom," Mike agreed.

Cindy noticed that the exquisite colt seemed to calm a little at Ian's touch. She could hardly wait to get to know the new gray horse better.

"Will he stay here at Saratoga?" she asked.

"For now," Ian said. "We'll probably take him home before the Belmont meet. He could ride down with you when Beth takes you back for school at the end of August."

At least that will be one good thing about going home. Cindy tried not to think how much she would miss Glory if he went on to Belmont to race and was away from home for months more. But it would be far worse if he lost his next race and returned to Kentucky in disgrace.

"When will Storm's Ransom start his yearling training?" she asked. Maybe soon she could put forward a plan she'd been thinking about since Wonder's Champion was born—to start seriously helping with the training and exercise riding of the young horses. Cindy knew that training wasn't a simple business. Her dad, Mike, and Ashleigh, the three licensed trainers on the farm, had spent years getting to where they were. But Ashleigh had started out training Wonder when she was twelve—just Cindy's age.

"Probably we'll start saddle-breaking him in September or October," Mike said. "It'll have to wait until I can get around to it. I'm going to have my hands full, since Ian will be staying at Belmont to look after our string there."

Good, Cindy said to herself. *It sounds like Mike is going to need help training.* Cindy looked thoughtfully at Storm's Ransom. The colt's bright eyes were fixed on her, as if he sensed they were going to mean a lot to each other.

"We haven't had a top-quality sprinter at Whitebrook since Blues King," Mike said.

"I'm looking forward to this, too," Ian added. "I used to train sprinters almost exclusively when my horses were in the allowance and claiming ranks."

"Storm's Ransom and Glory will look gorgeous galloping together!" Cindy could just imagine the dark and dapple gray horses going around the track at Whitebrook.

"Where's Tor?" Samantha asked, looking around. "I'd found him a minute ago. I think I outran him."

Cindy smiled. Samantha was in college, and most

of the time she acted like an adult. But when she got excited about something, she acted like a little kid again.

Cindy saw Tor's blond head coming toward them through the bustle of horses and handlers. "I stopped to talk to someone else who has a horse entered in the Turf Writers Steeplechase," Tor said. "Hi, everybody."

"Hi again," Samantha said with a smile. "How does the field for the Turf Writers look?"

"Sierra's not going to win the race going away— we're going to have to fight for it." Tor frowned. "Tomorrow morning I'll take him over fences. That terror," Tor added, the serious expression on his face melting into a grin.

"I've had Sierra out twice, but just once over fences. He did well," Samantha confirmed.

"The 'chase is in a week. We're right on schedule," Tor said.

Cindy didn't want to interrupt, but she could hardly wait to tell her news about Ben and Glory. "Guess what—I saw Ben Cavell here. He thinks Glory will go better if I ride him!"

"Where, honey?" Ian looked concerned. "You know you can't ride on the track."

"I don't know where yet." Cindy wished her father wouldn't look so skeptical. "But not on the track. Don't you think it's a good idea, Dad?"

"I want very much to hear what Ben has to say about the colt," Ian said quickly. "But honey, Ben hasn't been around Glory recently. I'm not sure he can just drop into the situation and solve the problem."

"Yeah, I guess," Cindy said reluctantly. "He said maybe we could all talk at dinner tonight. He'll call you."

"Okay, sweetie." Ian nodded.

"I'm going to see Sierra," Tor said. "Sammy, do you want to come?"

"Sure." Samantha squeezed Cindy's shoulder encouragingly as she passed.

Sierra had been a problem horse also, Cindy thought, but he had straightened out and become a champion. Cindy just hoped Ben's idea for Glory would work, too.

10

"We're going on a short trip," Ben said the next morning. He opened the door of Whitebrook's two-horse trailer so that Cindy could load Glory. "We'll be driving only a couple of hours. I think he'll be fine."

Cindy nodded. She could hardly suppress her excitement—she was going to ride Glory! The day was perfect for a ride. The morning cool still lingered in the air, clean from the previous day's rain, and a breeze ruffled the heavy leaves of the trees.

"Okay, Glory," Cindy said to the colt. "Time to go."

Glory looked at her, then obediently put first one and then the other foreleg on the wood surface of the trailer floor and hopped in. The trailer swayed, but Glory was accustomed to loading and stood quietly. As Cindy secured the gate behind him, she again tried to think where on earth Ben could be taking them for their ride.

At dinner the night before, she'd had a great time with Ben and her family at a Chinese restaurant.

They'd talked mostly about bloodlines, analyzing those of Storm's Ransom compared to Glory's. Ben regarded Glory as a miracle horse, the first successful breeding that had resulted in the passing on of the Just Victory superhorse characteristics of speed, stamina, and heart.

But all evening Ben had refused to tell Cindy where she was going the next day to ride Glory. He'd told her parents. Cindy could tell from her parents' and Ben's expressions that they thought she was in for a real treat. Ian and Mike seemed happy that Ben would be taking Glory—Cindy knew they were ready to try anything to get the colt back up to form. Ben had asked Samantha to come along, too.

Cindy shook her head, puzzled about the whole expedition. As far as she knew, just rolling countryside surrounded the track. Why was Ben taking them so far just to ride? Asking Samantha along added to the mystery. In strange terrain Cindy would need someone to ride with, but Ben would be there. He'd already said he planned to ride.

Cindy opened the front window of the trailer and looked in at Glory. The colt was bobbing his head as he tore off big chunks of hay from the sheaf she had stocked for him in the trailer.

"Are you ready for our adventure?" Cindy asked.

Glory stretched his neck so that he could touch her fingers with his muzzle. Cindy tickled its soft tip.

"Be careful in the trailer, boy," she cautioned as she shut the window. "Don't bump your head." Cindy walked to the back of the trailer to double-check the trailer's hitch with the truck. It was tightly fastened. She gave the colt's tail a final pat over the half-door.

"Do you have any idea what this is all about?" Samantha asked as she opened the passenger door to the truck. "Ben won't give me a clue—he just said he's sure I'll enjoy the trip as much as you will."

"Search me." Cindy shrugged, pulling Glory's bridle off her shoulder to stow in the tack compartment at the front of the trailer. "I mean, I know Ben's trying to get Glory to behave better on the track, and our trip has something to do with that."

"It's nice that a trainer of Ben's caliber stays so involved with Glory, Cindy," Samantha said seriously. "Ben obviously thinks Glory's worth a lot of trouble."

He's worth a lot of trouble—and he is *a lot of trouble,* Cindy thought wryly. Through the tinted glass of the trailer window she could see Glory peacefully eating his hay, as if they were going for a Sunday picnic. He really was an easygoing horse, she thought—unless he was approached the wrong way.

"Ready?" Ben asked.

"I sure am," Cindy said eagerly.

As Ben drove away from the track, Cindy looked out the window for signs of where they were going. The fenced green hills near Saratoga looked like horse country to her. But if Ben just wanted her to take Glory for a trail ride, that wouldn't be much of a surprise.

"Almost there," Ben said cheerfully. "Keep your eyes open."

For what? Cindy wondered. Gazing out the window, she saw luxuriant fields of emerald grass speckled with purple heads of clover. Here and there small herds of horses grazed. With their graceful builds they looked like Thoroughbreds to Cindy, but she was too far away to tell for sure.

Ben slowed the truck.

"Look!" Samantha gasped. "Oh, Cindy! Over there, in that field. I've never seen anything like it!"

"What?" Cindy stared out Samantha's window. "Oh, my gosh!" She drew in a sharp breath. In a paddock by the road a glorious black stallion was running alongside the fence. There was no mistaking that proudly crested neck and the powerful sweep of the stallion's strides as he galloped up and down the fence line, whinnying shrilly. "It's Just Victory!" Cindy cried.

"The one and only." Ben smiled.

From the trailer Glory whinnied back loudly to Just Victory. His call was identical to that of his grandsire's.

Cindy couldn't speak for a few moments. Samantha was silent, too. "I've never seen a horse like that," Samantha finally said in a hushed voice. "He's magnificent!"

"He still affects me like that, too," Ben said quietly. "Just Victory's seventeen, but he's in a class by himself."

Ben pulled up in the driveway of a gracious old stone house. Behind it Cindy caught a glimpse of several small stone barns. A slender, white-haired man in his seventies walked across the drive to greet them.

"Hi, Ben," he said. "It's been a while—since the spring meet at Hollywood Park, I think."

"That's right." The two men shook hands.

"Cindy and Samantha McLean, I'd like you to meet Richard Bullington," Ben introduced them. "Just Victory is his horse."

Cindy's eyes widened. This was the man who owned one of the greatest racehorses of all time. She could hardly believe she was being introduced to him. "H-How do you do," she stammered.

"Very well, thank you." Mr. Bullington smiled at Cindy and Samantha. "I've certainly wanted to meet you and everyone else at Whitebrook. March to Glory does Just Victory proud."

Cindy relaxed a little at the obvious sincerity in Mr. Bullington's voice. He wasn't a snobby celebrity. He was just someone who knew he'd had a once-in-a-lifetime opportunity to own a superhorse. Cindy couldn't help looking closely at Mr. Bullington. *I wonder what it feels like to have a horse like that*, she thought. *I still think I'll know someday with Glory.*

"Let's go into the barn," Mr. Bullington suggested. "I'll show you around."

Inside, the stone barn was swept clean. But there were a few forgotten pieces of tack in a corner, and dust covered the sills of the small, wood-framed windows. It seemed to Cindy that a kind of twilight had settled over the farm.

"This place looks old," Samantha said.

"It is," Mr. Bullington confirmed. "It's been in my family for over a hundred years. And we've been raising Thoroughbreds for almost that long. We've had a number of outstanding runners, but never a Just Victory—before or since."

Cindy didn't want to chatter like a small child, but she had so many questions for Mr. Bullington. "Do you miss seeing Just Victory race?" she asked.

"Not really—it's good to have him home." Mr. Bullington smiled. "His racing days were exciting, but seeing him every day is another kind of thrill."

A horse's hooves clattered loudly on the cement aisle. Cindy turned to see what horse it was, and her mouth dropped open. A groom was leading Just Victory toward them. The stallion was tossing his head and playfully grabbing at the rope.

"We'll get to see him close up?" Cindy asked breathlessly.

"Of course. He likes attention," Mr. Bullington said. "Why don't you go say hello? Randy, our head groom, will hold him."

Cindy slowly approached the stallion. She intended to be very careful. From watching Just Victory run in the pasture, she could tell that his temperament was different from Glory's. As she neared Just Victory she could see that the fire in the stallion's eyes was still fierce. Cindy put up her hand for Just Victory to sniff. "You are such a wonderful horse," she said quietly.

Just Victory leaned closer until his muzzle touched her hand. Then he jerked his head away. The stallion's ears went back a fraction.

"It's okay," Cindy soothed. "I know you're a spirited guy. I just want to get to know you. I ride your grandson, and he's as beautiful and spirited as you are."

The stallion's expression softened as Cindy talked to him. He stepped forward and pushed his muzzle firmly into her hands. He didn't seem to object as she slowly reached up to rub his ears.

Cindy marveled as she ran her hands over Just Victory's deep chest and down his slender legs. He had run so very fast once—so much faster than anyone had thought it possible for a horse to run.

She noticed that Randy was tacking up the stallion. "Are you going to ride him?" she asked Mr. Bullington.

"No, Samantha is," Ben interjected, smiling. "You're going to ride Glory, and I'll ride one of the other horses here. We'll go on a very special trail ride."

Samantha looked stunned. "I can't believe this," she said. "I must be dreaming that I'm going to ride Just Victory. But don't wake me up."

Cindy felt like jumping and whooping for joy. *I was right that we were going on a trail ride,* she thought. *I just didn't know the two greatest racehorses in the world were going, too!*

"We still ride Just Victory quite a bit," Randy explained. "It keeps him in shape."

"And he enjoys getting out so much," Mr. Bullington added. "Mostly Randy rides him, but occasionally I get on and dream of past glory." He winked at Cindy.

Glory whinnied loudly from his trailer. Cindy thought she detected a note of exasperation. "I'm coming, boy!" she called. "I'm sorry we're keeping you waiting."

Tearing herself away from Just Victory, Cindy hurried out to the colt. She clipped a lead rope to Glory's halter and carefully backed him out of the trailer. The colt immediately tugged on the line to get his head and began to graze on the rich grass surrounding the drive.

"He's making himself at home," Ben said, laughing.

"He always does." Glory had done so much traveling—to the Kentucky tracks in the spring, and in the summer to Belmont and Saratoga—that he settled right in wherever he was. Cindy hadn't expected this strange place to rattle him.

"How is Glory around other horses?" Randy asked as he led Just Victory out of the barn. The stallion was tacked up and ready for the ride. Samantha followed, looking happy and a little dazed.

"Glory's usually fine with other horses," Cindy said. "He's never tried to fight on the backside or the track." As if to prove her point, Glory kept his back to Just Victory and continued grazing, hardly seeming to notice his grandsire's presence.

Ben walked over from the trailer with Glory's tack. Glory gave an indignant snort as Ben threw the saddle over his back and cinched the girth.

"Sorry, guy, but it's time to work," Cindy said firmly, pulling up Glory's head from the grass. She didn't intend to let him get away with bad behavior that day. These days Glory seemed to think more

131

about grazing, hanging out in his stall and mooching carrots, and acting up than racing.

She easily slipped the bit into the colt's mouth and mounted up. As she gathered the reins, Cindy tried to gauge Glory's mood. She hadn't ridden him since the beginning of the summer. That was before he'd formed the bad habits that were causing so much trouble on the track.

But Glory stood quietly, awaiting her instructions as always. "That's a good boy," Cindy said. She leaned forward in the saddle, running her hands through Glory's thick mane. It felt wonderful to be on her horse again.

"Cindy, look at this!" Samantha called. She was circling Just Victory at a walk. The feisty stallion was pulling hard on the reins, but Samantha wasn't having trouble keeping him in hand. Cindy was sure Samantha could handle any horse after riding Sierra. Probably Ben had told Mr. Bullington that.

Ben rode up on a reddish chestnut gelding. The horse's quick, precise steps and arched, muscular neck indicated to Cindy that this was another finely bred animal. "Let's go," Ben said, reining his horse toward a lane between the side paddocks.

Cindy started to follow on Glory, but Just Victory imperiously pushed by them. Clearly he intended to be out in front even at a walk. Glory seemed startled. He increased his own pace to catch up.

"Have fun," Mr. Bullington called. Cindy thought the older man sounded wistful, as if he would like to join them.

Cindy settled back in the saddle, relishing riding her horse. The colt moved lightly and easily with his familiar rider.

"Can you believe this is us?" Samantha asked with a laugh.

"Not really!" Cindy grinned back.

She looked over at Just Victory, comparing him to Glory. Glory, at just over sixteen hands, was taller. Just Victory was barely over fifteen hands, but stocky and muscular. Cindy remembered that at the beginning of Just Victory's career, no one had thought a horse so short could ever be a champion—that had been said of Wonder, too.

Just Victory had a perfectly even blaze and two white stockings on his back legs. Even the stallion's white back hooves had been considered a disadvantage by many at first—white hooves were said to be softer and less able to stand up to the pounding of a race. Just Victory had proved them wrong about that, too.

The similarities between Glory and his grandsire, Cindy thought, were in the horses' finely shaped heads and wide-set, slightly prominent eyes. They moved the same way, too, with a flowing, effortless rippling of muscles. Just Victory was still leading the way, but Glory was right up at his flank, trying to pass him.

"Just Victory and Glory are a lot alike," Cindy said finally.

"Yes," Ben agreed. "The likeness is fairly subtle, but it's there. The moment I saw Glory, I knew I really had something."

"Which horse is that?" Cindy asked, pointing to Ben's horse.

"Canady Red."

Wow! Another multiple stakes winner, Cindy thought with excitement. She couldn't believe what a high-powered ride this was.

"We can let the horses out a little," Ben said. "Just Victory's well conditioned—Mr. Bullington thought a gallop would be good for him. Let's trot them."

Cindy squeezed with her legs, remembering from past rides exactly how much to cue the colt to ask for a trot. Glory instantly moved out at the faster gait. Cindy loved Glory's smooth trot. She posted, letting him quicken the pace until they had drawn even with Just Victory.

With an irritated snort at Glory's near approach, Just Victory broke into a gallop. Without being asked, Glory leaped into a gallop, too, as if he were breaking from a starting gate. He cut into Just Victory's lead until they were neck and neck.

Suddenly Just Victory roared into a full racing gallop and charged ahead. The stallion had moved into the higher gear in barely a second.

Cindy felt a moment of pure awe. She had just seen Just Victory's famous drive when he decided to put away his rivals. In his renowned Kentucky Derby run, where he won by twenty lengths, Just Victory had switched into overdrive in the stretch.

Almost without thinking, Cindy leaned over Glory's neck in a jockey's crouch, asking for speed.

With a snort of delight Glory responded, moving up beside his grandsire again.

Angrily pinning his ears at the challenge, Just Victory reached for ground. He was determined to win! The older horse drew off again.

For a second Glory hesitated, as if he were surprised. Then he laid back his ears as well. Both horses swept around a curve in the lane at racing speed.

Now Cindy could see that Just Victory's beautiful, perfect stride at a run was exactly like Glory's. The cool breeze whipped Cindy's blond hair across her face as she kneaded her hands along Glory's neck, asking again for speed. Glory responded like the wind!

Cindy could feel Glory's urgent need to win. The colt's ears were pinned flat against his head as they flew up the lane.

Glancing over, Cindy saw Samantha's excited, happy face. Cindy laughed aloud. This was living— nothing could ever top this ride!

"Pull them up!" Ben called from behind them. "Just Victory hasn't raced in over ten years!"

Ben was right, Cindy realized. Quickly she rose in the stirrups, asking Glory to slow. He didn't want to—finally she had to circle him until he dropped back into a slow gallop, then a high-stepping, excited trot.

"Too bad nobody had a stopwatch," Samantha said with a grin. She was circling the black stallion, too. "This guy can still really turn on the speed."

"So can Glory." Cindy looked down at the colt. He

was barely winded. The reason he was losing races and putting in bad works definitely wasn't a physical problem.

"We'd better walk them out and head back," Ben said. "We can always visit again."

"I'd love to! This was the best ride ever." Cindy couldn't stop smiling.

After they had thanked Mr. Bullington again at the barn, Ben drove them to the track. Cindy was quiet most of the way. Her mind was too full of her ride and of Just Victory's classic beauty for speech. *I've just seen the greatest horse that ever lived and gone on a ride with him,* she thought in wonder. *I'll never forget this day, even if I live to be a hundred.*

Samantha looked over at Cindy. "So how did Glory go?" she asked. "He looked great to me out there."

"He seems to be himself again," Cindy said hopefully. "Maybe he'll behave on the track now."

11

Cindy stood at the rail on Tuesday, watching a new jockey work Glory on the track. It was just before dawn, and a light fog the color of Glory's coat almost obscured the colt. When the gray horse was on the far side of the track, Cindy could barely see him as he moved in and out of streamers of mist.

What she did see of the work looked terrible. Glory was galloping erratically along the track, trying to get his head and veering off on crazy diagonals. Then abruptly he slacked off the bit, slowing as dramatically as if he were sight-seeing.

Cindy ground her teeth in frustration. How could Glory do this? she wondered. Just four days earlier he'd gone perfectly when she had ridden him with Just Victory.

This was Glory's last work before the Travers on Saturday. Donny McGovern, a well-known jockey who was currently leading in earnings at Saratoga, was up on the colt. But Cindy had known the work wouldn't go well from the minute Glory started skittering sideways at the warm-up trot.

Glory drifted toward the rail as he galloped around the clubhouse turn. Cindy knew that Glory always tended to lug in a little. He almost seemed to understand that by keeping near the rail, he could take the shortest distance around the track.

But he'd nearly hit it! Cindy gasped in shock. Donny barely managed to right the colt.

"Glory's at it again," Mike said grimly. Ian watched in silence, his mouth set in a tense line.

"I know." Cindy willed the colt to settle down. *Don't do this, Glory,* she thought. *You're going to get killed!*

Glory lurched into the backstretch, short-striding. Cindy was surprised that a rider as skilled as Donny was having so much trouble with the colt. Glory was really being a handful.

The big gray horse swept around the far turn. Cindy nodded nervously—now Glory seemed to be going all right. His stride was more relaxed, and he was moving in a straight line. Maybe, she thought, he was remembering from his last race that when he came into the stretch, it was time to settle down or lose.

The next second Glory skidded sharply toward the rail. "Stop him!" Cindy screamed. But Glory had stopped himself, so sharply that he unseated Donny. The jockey tumbled over Glory's head and hit the turf. Cindy stared at the track in shock. She couldn't believe how quickly the accident had happened.

Donny was on his feet in an instant. He waved his crop.

"He's okay!" Mike said. "Here comes Glory. He doesn't seem to be injured, either."

Glory was rushing for the wire, riderless again. Cindy breathed a huge sigh of relief. She doubted Glory could move at that pace if he had seriously hurt himself. He must have missed the rail.

"Cindy, will you try to get Glory?" Mike asked. "He might come to you the quickest."

"Be careful, honey," Ian said anxiously.

"I will." Feeling an awful sense of déjà vu, Cindy looked both ways and ran out onto the track, just as she had when Ashleigh fell. This time four riders coming onto the stretch hadn't seen the accident or slowed. They swept by the wire at a flat-out run. Cindy stopped in the middle of the track to let them pass.

She heard the muffled thunder of hooves digging deep into the soft surface as the horses flew by her. They passed so close, she could feel a fine spray of sandy dirt on her face.

When they had gone around the turn, Cindy saw that an escort rider, a young woman riding a Quarter Horse, had caught Glory and was bringing him back. The colt was walking obediently behind the other horse and seemed subdued. Maybe the walk back had calmed him, Cindy thought.

I hope he's not hurt! She ran up the track as fast as she could on the freshly harrowed surface.

"Here he is," said the escort rider.

"Thank you." Cindy caught Glory's reins. Glory was trembling all over. He urgently bumped her with his nose.

"Take a look at his left side," the escort rider said, sounding concerned. "I think he hit the rail."

Cindy felt the color drain out of her face as she walked to Glory's other side. "Oh, Glory!" she cried. The colt had a long mark on his side where brushing the rail had rubbed away his coat.

Cindy knew the scratch was only superficial, but she hated to see her beloved horse hurt in any way. She was shaking and near tears. Glory had come so close to having a terrible accident.

Ian and Mike were standing on the track near the gap, watching them with worried faces.

"He scuffed the rail," she called.

Both men immediately ran over to examine the colt. Cindy stood beside them, her eyes wide with worry.

"It's not serious." Cindy could see the relief on Mike's face as he gently touched Glory's side above the scratch. "Thank heaven he didn't hang himself up on the rail or injure his legs."

"But this isn't good," Ian said with a sigh. "Glory could have caused a serious accident out there. Despite his reputation, if he doesn't settle down, he may be asked to leave the track altogether."

He definitely won't win the Travers if he can't go on the track. Cindy looked at her horse. Glory had lowered his head and was standing completely still. The accident had badly shaken him.

"I'll take him back to the barn and dress the scratch," Len said gently, coming up behind them.

"Thanks." Cindy stared out at the track, where Glory was so conspicuously absent. Tears of frustration burned her eyes.

Cindy leaned on the rail and tried to compose herself, but it was hard. She was living her worst nightmare.

Donny was walking slowly toward them, dusting off his jeans.

"Are you really okay?" Mike asked with concern.

"Yeah, fine. I missed the rail and went into the grass." Donny shrugged and looked after Glory. "Is he all right?"

"We think so," Mike said.

"I'll try riding again if you want," Donny offered. "For a couple of seconds out there he was going okay."

Cindy knew that all the top jockeys at the track were eager to ride Glory, despite the problems they were having with him. Glory had already set a track record and won almost all his races—he was a remarkable horse. If he ran well, the jockey stood to have a fantastic ride or even a stakes or world record to his credit.

"Thank you, Donny, but that would be pointless." Ian ran a hand through his hair. "The colt can't run in the Travers," he said to Mike. "Not after that performance. We'd be kidding ourselves if we tried."

Cindy started to protest, but she saw how discouraged her dad looked as he and Mike turned to go back to the barn. She was more worried than ever when she saw Donny limping away, holding his rib cage. He was obviously hurt more than he'd let on—riding Glory was starting to be very dangerous, Cindy realized.

"What happened?" Samantha asked Cindy as she led Matchless up to the track for his morning work. She gestured at Donny.

"Glory threw him," Cindy said hopelessly. "Donny almost went into the rail. Glory did hit it, but I don't think he's badly hurt."

"What are we going to do with that guy?" Samantha mused.

"I don't know." Cindy shrugged. "I guess take him back to Whitebrook. Dad doesn't want Glory to run in the Travers after what happened today. Maybe at home Len and Ashleigh and I can turn him around." Cindy sighed unhappily. She imagined how dreary it would be around Whitebrook when she and Glory went home in disgrace. *But we'll still have each other,* she thought fiercely. *I don't care what anyone thinks.*

"Look who's coming!" Samantha said. Cindy glanced at her sister's bright expression, then looked behind her. Glory was coming back up to the track. The colt's step was springy, and he was tossing his head eagerly.

Cindy's eyes widened with delight, and not just because Glory had perked up. Ashleigh was leading him!

"Hey, Sammy and Cindy." Ashleigh waved.

"Ashleigh! You're back!" Cindy almost burst into

tears from sheer relief. Ashleigh was wearing maternity clothes now instead of her usual jeans or riding breeches, but her brisk walk and air of control were the same.

"Yes, I finally finished up with the Townsends in Kentucky," Ashleigh said. "We struck a deal about Wonder's Champion." Suddenly Ashleigh's expression darkened.

Cindy opened her mouth to ask what had happened with the Townsends, but Ashleigh's look stopped her. *I'll find out later,* she thought. *Right now I need Ashleigh's help with Glory!* "Why is Glory back?" Cindy asked. "Didn't you hear what happened this morning?"

"I did," Ashleigh confirmed. "I brought Glory back because I had an idea about what to try with him. He's not really hurt—Len and I dressed his scratch, and I think he can go out again. We're going to put a new jockey up. I just told Mike and Ian."

"Who?" Cindy asked. She couldn't suppress a surge of hope at Ashleigh's words, even though Ian and Mike had tried a dozen jockeys already.

"Felipe Aragon." Ashleigh was looking Glory over minutely.

"But that's Flightful's jockey!" Cindy said in astonishment. How could the jockey of Glory's archrival ride Glory?

"Felipe's decided to ride for us instead of for Joe Gallagher," Ashleigh said. "He'd rather have a chance to ride Glory, and he wants to be based on the East Coast."

Cindy gasped. Joe Gallagher, the trainer who had tried to have Glory killed at Belmont, would be furious about Whitebrook's stealing his jockey, she was sure. *I hope he doesn't try again to hurt Glory because of this,* Cindy worried. *But I guess he can't, now that we're watching out for him.*

"Felipe's very good," Ashleigh continued. "He also rides according to instruction. If we tell him how we want Glory ridden, he'll do it. I think the other jockeys we tried pursued their own riding styles and didn't really listen to what we had to say about Glory's special requirements. Or they just weren't intuitive enough to respond to a horse as sensitive as he is."

"Hey, Ashleigh." Felipe Aragon walked up, smiling. "So I get to try the big one." He nodded at Glory.

"I'd like you to," Ashleigh said. "I don't know how closely you've been following Glory's races and works—"

"Very closely," Felipe interrupted. "I've always wanted a chance to ride this guy. Who doesn't?"

"Then you know what he's been up to," Ashleigh said. "Glory can't be ridden in a ham-handed way, but he has to know you mean business. He takes a lot of riding out there, but the result can certainly be impressive."

"No doubt about that. Let me try him the way we talked about last night." Felipe took Glory's reins from Len and mounted up. Cindy watched him ride off, her heart in her throat. She wondered what Ashleigh's instructions to Felipe had been. *This just has to work,* she thought.

Mike and Ian had returned from the barn and stood quietly beside Ashleigh. "I wouldn't put Glory back out on the track for anyone but you," Ian said to Ashleigh.

"He's going well now." Ashleigh picked up her binoculars. "Here come Matchless and Samantha. I suggested that we work Glory with another horse to wake him up. That's worked in the past."

It's a good idea, Cindy thought. Glory had certainly woken up when he'd raced against Just Victory.

The morning fog had burned off, and Cindy could see Glory clearly now under the spilling yellow light of the August sun. The colt was testing Felipe to the limit, trying to bolt after another horse. Felipe kept him in hand, but he didn't fight him.

"Good, good," Cindy murmured. Felipe was already doing better than Kelly Morgan and some of the other jockeys they'd tried on Glory.

Glory rounded the far turn, slowing into a lazy gallop. Cindy groaned silently. Glory was up to his old tricks.

"Here comes Matchless." Ashleigh's hazel eyes were narrowed with concentration. "Now we'll see if Glory kicks in."

The chestnut colt was roaring up on the inside. For a frozen second Matchless was out in front, coming into the stretch.

Then Glory saw the other colt. In a fraction of a second he switched gears, his strides covering huge amounts of ground. Glory blazed across the finish!

Samantha flew by the wire on Matchless, five

lengths behind. She gave Cindy a grin and a thumbs-up.

"I guess we're going to be racing in four days after all!" Ian said. He sounded stunned.

Mike smiled broadly. "Thanks, Ashleigh. I guess I'll know who to call the next time I have a problem horse."

"Well, don't plan the victory celebration yet," Ashleigh cautioned. "That was a decent work but not an outstanding one. Matchless caught Glory napping. Glory overpowered him because Matchless isn't in Glory's class as a racehorse. But Glory's going to have to do much better than that to win against the grade-one competition in the Travers."

"Still, I'm very relieved," Ian said. "Race day will be Felipe's second ride on Glory. Probably the colt will go even better for him."

"I hope so." Ashleigh nodded. "Felipe really has a way of getting inside a horse's mind. I just wish it hadn't taken me so long to think of him."

"Why did you?" Mike asked.

Felipe was turning Glory at a slow gallop. The big colt seemed to be minding the jockey perfectly, as if to say, *Now I don't have to prove anything.*

"I spent a lot of time thinking about different jockeys' riding styles, and it seemed to me Felipe's would fit Glory," Ashleigh said. "But of course he was in California riding for Joe Gallagher and other trainers out there. Then I remembered overhearing Felipe say that he wished he were based in New York, where most of his family is, instead of California. And he'd said a lot of positive things about Glory." Ashleigh shrugged. "All of a sudden the information just clicked. I realized it would at least be worth a phone call to see if he was interested in riding for us."

"It sure was!" Cindy smiled as Felipe rode up on Glory. She took Glory's reins and patted the colt's damp neck. "I'm so proud of you, big guy!"

Glory blissfully rubbed his ears against her shirt, as if he were satisfied with himself as well.

"Nice one, Felipe," Mike said. "Thanks."

"No problem." Felipe touched his crop to his helmet. "See you on Saturday, if not before."

"Come on, Glory," Cindy said. "Let's get you cooled out and give you a treat. Today you really deserve one."

As if he understood, Glory pulled at the reins urgently in the direction of the barn.

"I'll walk back with you," Ashleigh said to Cindy. "Then we can talk."

"Great!" As they threaded their way through the hot-walkers, riders, and grooms leading horses to and from the track, Cindy looked over at Ashleigh. She wondered if Ashleigh felt any different now that her pregnancy had progressed to the point where she was wearing maternity clothes.

"I'm having a perfect pregnancy so far," Ashleigh said with a smile, seeing Cindy's glance. "I really feel even better than usual. Of course, it's hard not being able to ride—I miss that terribly. But I have so many administrative things to do at Whitebrook, maybe it's just as well."

"When do you have to go back?" Cindy asked. Ashleigh looked so troubled, she thought. Maybe the deal about Wonder's Champion still wasn't completely worked out. Cindy wondered again what the Townsends had agreed to with Ashleigh about the colt.

"I'll go back to Whitebrook with Mike in a couple of days—I thought I'd stay here through the Travers," Ashleigh said. "It's a little iffy to have all of us here, with no one but the stable hands looking out for the horses at home."

"Thanks for staying, Ashleigh," Cindy said gratefully. She knew they'd be lucky if they didn't run into more snags with Glory before race day. Having Ashleigh around might make all the difference.

Ashleigh frowned. "Don't thank me yet," she said.

"Why?" Cindy looked at her in surprise. She had no idea what could be bothering Ashleigh. "Everything is going so incredibly well," she said. "I guess Mike has told you. I mean, Shining won the Whitney, Four Leaf Clover sold for so much to a wonderful farm, and now Glory's going to win his next race!" She ran her hand lovingly along Glory's sleek gray neck. The colt nudged her back.

Ashleigh looked worried. "All of that's great—in fact, it couldn't be better. But Cindy, there's something I need to tell you. It's about Glory."

Cindy swallowed nervously. She could tell that what was coming was big—and not good.

"You know that I want to train Wonder's Champion at Whitebrook," Ashleigh began.

Cindy nodded quickly. "Yes, of course," she said. "The Townsends are willing to let me do that—"

"That's so great!" Cindy interrupted joyfully. She couldn't believe the Townsends had given in already about where Wonder's Champion would stay. Cindy had expected the argument to drag out until the next year, when the colt began his yearling training.

Ashleigh held up a hand. "Wait. I had to give them something in return."

Cindy was silent. Her heart began to pound with fear.

Ashleigh looked at the ground for a moment. "I don't know how to say this to make it any easier on you."

Cindy tightened her grip on Glory's lead line. *Just tell me*, she pleaded silently. *Not knowing is worse.*

"I've given the Townsends a half interest in Glory," Ashleigh said.

12

"No!" Cindy gasped. "You can't!"

"I already did." Ashleigh looked sad but resigned. "I discussed this with Ian and Mike before I signed the legal papers. The half interest in Glory is the only thing the Townsends will accept in exchange for our training Wonder's Champion at Whitebrook. Brad in particular was adamant about the deal."

"But Glory hasn't even been running very well," Cindy said desperately. Her mind was working fast, trying to find a way out. This just couldn't be true, she thought. Not after everything she'd gone through to get the colt for Whitebrook.

"I know he hasn't, but the Townsends can see beyond this temporary setback to Glory's true potential." Ashleigh was looking at her intently, as if she was trying to figure out a way to soften the blow. "Not only as a racehorse, but as a sire," she went on. "Glory is the first of Just Victory's offspring that seems capable of continuing the line of champions."

Cindy opened her mouth to argue some more—and shut it. *What's the use?* she thought miserably. She could see that it was hopeless. The deal was done.

"Look, I didn't just give him away," Ashleigh said gently. "It's only a half interest. I've had an unusual arrangement with the Townsends about Mr. Wonderful, where they're technically his owners so that I can be his jockey. That's worked out well so far. According to the agreement the Townsends and I reached about Glory, he'll stay at Whitebrook for training. And we'll continue to do the training. Nothing will change."

Cindy didn't believe it. She was sure the Townsends would interfere with Glory. They always had with every other horse Whitebrook and Townsend Acres co-owned. Besides, why would they want to own half of him if they weren't planning to have a say in his training and racing?

"When we retire Glory to stud, Townsend Acres will get some breeding rights," Ashleigh said, as if she were reading Cindy's mind. "That could be worth millions if Glory reaches the potential in his racing career that we all think he will. And although it's not foolproof, there's a chance he'll pass on the Just Victory characteristics of speed, stamina, and courage. Having breeding rights to a stallion with those characteristics is enough for the Townsends, Cindy. I don't think they're going to interfere with Glory's training. That was disastrous in the past."

"Sure," Cindy said weakly. She couldn't be angry with Ashleigh. She understood why Ashleigh had given the half interest in Glory to the Townsends. Otherwise Princess, Mr. Wonderful, and Pride would have to leave Whitebrook. Cindy couldn't think of another way to keep Wonder's Champion at Whitebrook, either. But she felt terrible.

"Don't worry about it right now," Ashleigh advised. "The Townsends are away until Saturday. Let's enjoy Sierra's run in the Turf Writers 'chase today. We can talk some more about this later."

Glory runs in the Travers on Saturday, Cindy thought. The Townsends were coming back to watch *their* horse—Glory. She just couldn't get used to the idea.

And I've got to leave the track the day after the Travers to go back to school. Cindy turned to Glory, running her hand lightly over his sleek gray shoulder. The colt was stepping quickly toward the barn, oblivious to the bad news. A lump rose in her throat. *I won't even be here to keep an eye on him,* she thought.

That afternoon Cindy sat in the clubhouse with her family, Mike, and Ashleigh, watching the eight-horse field go to the post for the New York Turf Writers Steeplechase. Cindy had said hardly a word since morning. She was afraid that if she opened her mouth, she would burst into tears. Samantha, Beth, and Ian kept glancing at her sympathetically, but nothing could make Cindy feel any better. Even the gorgeous day, glittering under a hot, bright sun, was mostly lost on her.

"The turf course is listed as firm," Samantha said to Cindy. "That's good for Sierra. His only losses have been on soft courses." Samantha smiled. "He's not a mud hog like Glory."

Cindy just nodded. She had never seen a steeplechase, and if she hadn't been heartbroken about Glory, she would have been looking forward to it. Sierra had been running in steeplechases for two years, since he was three. Now he was one of the top steeplechasers in the country. He would almost certainly put on a good show that day.

The Thoroughbreds making their way to the inner turf course were beautiful, well-bred horses. Cindy knew that many of them, including Sierra, had done badly racing on the flat but had proven to be extremely talented at steeplechasing.

Sierra, prancing lightly and skittering, was the picture of coiled energy. Tor wore the blue-and-white racing silks of Whitebrook, and he had a tense but determined expression on his face. Both horse and rider looked good, Cindy thought.

"This is a big race," Mike said, leaning around Ian to talk to Samantha. "I guess steeplechases are worth our while after all." He winked.

"I'm glad everybody thinks so now," Samantha joked. Cindy knew that two years earlier, when Sierra had failed dismally at flat racing, Mike had wanted to wash his hands of the colt and sell him to a breeder in Florida. But after Sierra took several freestyle fences, one a paddock fence and the other a six-foot tree when he bolted on a trail ride with Samantha, Samantha and Tor were convinced Sierra had talent as a jumper.

They'd had to convince Mike, who had been dubious about getting into steeplechasing at Whitebrook. With reason, he had argued that it was a sport none of them knew anything about. But he'd let Samantha and Tor try to prepare Sierra for steeplechasing, using Whitebrook's facilities. They'd pooled their knowledge of racing and jumping and trained Sierra to the level he was at now.

"Are you ever going to ride in another steeplechase?" Cindy asked her sister.

Samantha laughed. "Not unless Tor breaks his arm again!" Several years earlier Tor had broken his arm right before Sierra's first steeplechase. In a dramatic switch of jockeys, Samantha had taken the reins and ridden Sierra to a fast-closing second, beating out riders and horses with far more experience than they.

"Why not?" Cindy asked.

"I don't really have time right now, with college. You have to take riding in steeplechases seriously—it's a fast-paced, dangerous sport. But riding in that one 'chase on Sierra was a thrill," Samantha admitted.

"We should all take steeplechasing more seriously—it's even more ritzy than flat racing," Mike said with a grin. "Some of the participants have been accused of catering their tailgate lunches. Tor might request a catered lunch after his ride, Ashleigh. Maybe you should order him one now."

"Please." Ashleigh laughed and pulled at her thick hair. "I have enough trouble putting up with the pretensions of the Townsends without serving up Brie and caviar to Tor. Don't let *him* start in on me, too."

"Steeplechasing's the sport of kings," Samantha murmured.

Ashleigh smiled. "Maybe in merry old England."

"An elaborate lunch might be fun once," Beth protested.

Cindy couldn't join in the fun. The mere mention of the Townsends made her stomach queasy.

She looked out at the track. The horses were approaching the start. The steeplechase would be run on Saratoga's seven-furlong inner turf course.

"Want to hear a little about steeplechasing?" Samantha asked her.

"Sure." Cindy was curious about the sport. *Besides, anything's better than thinking about Glory belonging to the Townsends*, she thought bitterly.

"The race is two and three-eighths miles," Samantha said.

"That's a long race!" Cindy was stunned. Even the Belmont Stakes, the third jewel of the Triple Crown, was only a mile and a half. The Belmont was considered a real test of a Thoroughbred's stamina. All of Glory's races so far had been at a mile and a quarter or less.

"The Turf Writers is a very long race," Samantha agreed. "These horses aren't just flops at flat racing, even if that's how they started out. They definitely have other talents."

"That's for sure," Cindy said, remembering Sierra's recent jump out of the paddock at Whitebrook.

"The race will be run over national fences, which are fifty-four inches high and made of steel and plastic," Samantha continued. "Some steeplechases are run over timber fences on a hunt course. The horses running in steeplechases are usually about four to eight years old, which is older than most flat racers. The jockeys are bigger, too. The average weight is about a hundred forty pounds."

Cindy glanced out at the track. At that moment Sierra pulled back his lips and snaked out his head toward the nearest horse.

"He's going to bite!" Beth said with alarm.

But Tor had anticipated Sierra's move and expertly shifted him aside. Sierra took a chunk out of the air.

"Sierra's up to form," Mike said dryly.

"He just feels good. He doesn't even land most of his nips," Samantha defended him.

Despite herself, Cindy smiled. In some ways Mike still considered Sierra a dubious prospect. But Samantha had always had a special bond with the difficult horse.

Mike scanned the field with his binoculars. "See that bay? Isn't that Fencing Time, Sammy?"

"Yep," Samantha confirmed. "He's a great horse—he's one of the few horses who's ever beaten Sierra in a 'chase. But he lost thirteen races on the flat before his owners decided to try him over fences."

Cindy was getting more and more interested in the race. "Which horse is that?" she asked, pointing to a well-muscled black, circling at a trot.

"That's Liverpool's Song. He was a bargain—his owner got him for just two thousand dollars." Samantha was gazing through her binoculars, too.

"He's been moving up steadily in the national standings and is going in as the second favorite after Sierra."

"Do you think Sierra will win?" Cindy asked.

"Oh, you know me—I'm always nervous before any race our horses are in, no matter what the odds," Samantha replied. "But I think he should win, barring disaster. Unfortunately disasters are common in steeplechasing—even more so than in flat racing."

Cindy looked quickly at Samantha to see if that was a joke. But her sister wasn't smiling. Cindy wondered if she was worried about Tor.

The horses had lined up at the start on the far side of the track. Cindy leaned forward excitedly in her seat as the flag dropped, signaling the eight horses to run. Sierra leaped from a standstill into a full gallop, powering toward the first fence a length ahead of Liverpool's Song. Almost before Cindy had time to think, Sierra roared over the fence in a blinding crush of horses. The horses were crowded so closely together, Cindy could scarcely distinguish which was which. They whipped around the first turn.

"How does Tor have time to figure out Sierra's approach to the jumps?" Cindy asked Samantha. Tor had taught Cindy a little about jumping, but she'd never tried to take an entire course of jumps at racing speed.

"He and Sierra both figure it out," Samantha said. "The approach is different for every jump." Samantha's eyes were glued to the track. "It's not like in stadium jumping, where the riders can walk the course and know exactly how many strides are between jumps. These jumps aren't that high, and so Tor can go for a lot of speed in between."

"Tor and Sierra are still ahead!" Cindy cried.

"But that's only the first fence," Samantha said. "They've got eleven to go."

The words had hardly left her mouth before the two lead horses had gathered, lifted, and hit the ground again. On the landing Sierra was still a length ahead of Liverpool's Song. One horse was dropping back, but the six others pounded at Sierra's flanks.

"Are most steeplechases this close?" Cindy asked breathlessly.

"No. But it's early yet—a lot can happen." Samantha's voice was clipped with tension.

Cindy sat back in her seat, wondering what was yet to come. Probably some of the horses would tire, she thought as they leaped over jump after jump. From her exercise riding Cindy could estimate the incredible stamina the steeplechasers would need to take twelve jumps at that speed over two and three-eighths miles.

Liverpool's Song had gained ground on Sierra after a stupendous jump, and Fencing Time had begun to inch up, too, Cindy noted with alarm. The two horses were almost tied with Sierra for the lead as the horses raced by the finish for the first time. Sweat had begun to darken their necks, and the race wasn't half over.

Tor was keeping Sierra where he was, just in the

lead, not yet asking him for more. Liverpool's Song and Fencing Time were right up with Sierra as they raced into the backstretch.

Then Sierra began to gain on his rivals, first by a neck, then by almost a length. "Sierra's pulling away!" Cindy said.

"I think that was Sierra's idea." Mike frowned slightly. "I wouldn't have expected Tor to put away the competition quite so soon."

I bet Sierra's got this race in the bag, Cindy thought confidently as the horses plunged around the course with Sierra still holding on to a small lead. She didn't see what could go wrong for the Whitebrook horse now. If the jumps were higher, Cindy might have worried Sierra would miss one, but she knew what he was capable of. Those fences were considerably lower than the paddock board ones that Sierra flew over with such ease.

The three leading horses again approached a fence nearly together. Just before takeoff Fencing Time's jockey tried to angle his mount through a small opening on the rail.

That won't work! Cindy just had time to think before Fencing Time caught the fence with his hind legs. In midair the bay horse began to twist, falling toward Sierra's hindquarters as the three horses hurtled over the jump. Liverpool Song's jockey yanked his horse's head to the side in midjump to avoid the falling horse.

But Tor hadn't seen what was happening behind him, Cindy thought frantically. The next second

Fencing Time's head smashed into Sierra's hindquarters. Thrown badly off balance, Sierra fell to his knees coming off the jump. Fencing Time went down completely, falling on his side. His head slammed into the turf.

Cindy stared at the field in horror. The wreck couldn't be that bad—but it was. And the rest of the pack was coming up fast behind the leaders. Most of the riders managed to guide their horses into the jump so that they would land around the accident, but the rider of Destiny's Blues, a tall chestnut, was trapped in between horses. He took the jump headed straight for the fallen horses.

At that instant Sierra found his feet again and roared on, pounding at the heels of Liverpool's Song. But Fencing Time was still down, struggling to rise, as Destiny's Blues soared into the air.

"Miss him!" Cindy cried, wringing her hands. "Oh, no!"

Destiny's Blues landed off the jump right behind Fencing Time and tripped over the fallen horse. He fell, too, spilling his rider.

Cindy was sure that both of the horses that were down, and probably the second rider, were dead or badly injured from the severe collision. But to her amazement, both jockeys and Destiny's Blues got quickly on their feet. Fencing Time's jockey was gently pulling on his horse's reins, urging him to stand.

Cindy couldn't believe it. In a blink two horses were out of the race. Sierra, who had been almost effortlessly in the lead, was fighting to catch the field as the horses circled the track for the second time. The entire makeup of the race had changed.

"That was excellent riding by Liverpool Song's jockey," Samantha said. "Now Fencing Time is up. I think both the horses and the riders are okay, except for bumps and bruises."

"It's a rough sport." Ian shook his head.

"Fencing Time's jockey, Cal Hansen, was recently suspended for a day because of reckless riding," Ashleigh remarked. "I'd say the ruling was justified."

Cindy looked anxiously out at the course. Sierra had closed with a rush over two fences, but he still had a lot of ground to make up. Liverpool's Song was in the lead, strongly galloping for the finish.

But Cindy knew that Sierra had never given up in a steeplechase. The dark chestnut horse seemed to be concentrating perfectly on Tor's commands as he thrust forward. Slowly he closed the gap with the black horse.

"I don't know if Sierra can catch Liverpool's Song. Liverpool had a better last fence, and Sierra's almost out of time," Mike said. He sounded worried.

"Yes, but Sierra's not a former flat racer for nothing," Samantha said excitedly. "He'll make up a lot of ground in the stretch!"

Samantha was right, Cindy saw. Sierra took the last fence almost together with Liverpool, finding his footing instantly on the landing. Then he switched into racing gear!

Cindy jumped to her feet with everyone else in the

stands, cheering. "Go, Sierra!" she screamed. "Dust them!"

Sierra didn't need any encouragement. With a toss of his head he accelerated still more, drawing clear of Liverpool's Song. Sierra crossed the finish to win by three lengths.

"Only two seconds off the course record." Ian smiled broadly.

"It's incredible that Sierra came back like that after the time he lost in the fall," Ashleigh said in amazement. "I doubt if his knees are completely sound, either."

"Whitebrook horses never quit." Samantha's eyes were shining. She turned to Cindy. "Just think, we'll be sitting here in four days watching Glory win."

Cindy sat back in her seat with a jolt. For about ten minutes she had forgotten about Glory, but now the whole terrible situation came back to her in a rush. Sierra was a great horse, but he had won because Tor rode him so well and because Tor and Samantha had devoted hours to training him right.

The Townsends were away just then, but what would they do to Glory when they got back? Cindy thought. Glory was such a sensitive, special horse. What if the Townsends changed everything around for him just when Ashleigh had found a winning combination?

13

"Where did this wind come from?" Beth asked, snatching her floppy straw hat just as it was about to bounce down the grandstand.

"I don't know. It wasn't predicted on the weather report last night." Cindy scanned the field with her binoculars. Glory had just entered the track for the post parade of the Travers that Saturday, with Felipe Aragon up.

Felipe put Glory into a trot, then an easy gallop, moving clockwise around the track. Glory was going well for Felipe—at least for the moment, Cindy thought.

She had to admit that despite her case of nerves about Glory, so far the day had been fine. Felipe had come by the barn early that morning and had a long strategy session with Ashleigh about how he should ride the race. Cindy had overheard some of it while she was grooming Glory, since Felipe and Ashleigh were talking right outside the stall.

"In the Jim Dandy and recent training, Glory hasn't been focused," Ashleigh had said. "He's drifted and dropped off the bit, and he's been caught by closers. I think you have to be careful that he doesn't get way out front at the beginning of the race. Kelly let him do that, and it was a mistake. Not because Glory might use himself up if he sets a fast pace, but because at this point Glory may need another horse to run against. At the same time you'll have to use your judgment about how much to rate him to keep him back with the other horses. I don't think he'll fight you, but he's used to being on the lead."

Felipe had listened, but he hadn't said much. Cindy hoped he would be able to follow Ashleigh's instructions. She knew that horse races were unpredictable—the Travers might not play out anything like the way Ashleigh had envisioned. But Ashleigh had walked away from Felipe looking optimistic.

Glory had looked good, too, after his thorough brushing, Cindy thought. Clearly he had known that it was race day. The big colt was even more alert than usual, and when she had left the stall, he was looking eagerly over the door, as if he could hardly wait to get out on the track. Cindy had noticed that Glory always seemed to know when a race was ahead that day. His food had been cut that morning, but Cindy was sure he also picked up on the subtle currents of excitement coming from herself and everyone else around him.

Cindy had been dreading the return of the Townsends for four days, since the moment Ashleigh had told her about the deal she'd struck with them about Glory. But Cindy's first taste of the new arrangement hadn't been bad. Mr. Townsend had come by the barn shortly after Felipe left. He had been gracious and reassuring about Glory. He had thanked Cindy for all her hard work with the colt and acknowledged that Glory needed special handling. "We won't make any of the mistakes of the past," Mr. Townsend had said, smiling. Cindy found herself smiling back.

Glory had acted like a pro in the saddling paddock, and he seemed to be behaving himself in the post parade. *Now*, Cindy thought, *we just have to see how he acts in the race.*

She bit a nail and tried to judge Glory's mood. She had no doubt that Felipe was a great rider, but he had worked Glory only once. And Glory had used up all his chances to lose—he almost surely had to win this race to go to the Breeders' Cup.

The horses were approaching the gate. Adieu, the black colt who had beaten Glory in the Jim Dandy, was walking quietly after the gate attendant in the number-one position. Cindy frowned.

"That's a good position for Adieu, isn't it?" she asked Ashleigh.

Ashleigh nodded. "Today it is, with the way the track's favoring the rail. But Glory's in the number-four hole—that's not bad, either."

"How do you think the wind will affect the race?" Cindy asked. A gust almost snatched the words out of her mouth.

"The time will probably be slow, since it's a head-wind." Ashleigh squinted thoughtfully at the track. "Some of the horses may spook—look at all the leaves and debris that are starting to blow onto the track. How do you think Glory will handle it?"

"I'm not sure." Cindy thought most horses were more nervous on windy days. Usually Glory wasn't. He'd won two races going away on blowing days, but never when the wind was so intense. This was practically a hurricane. Cindy grabbed her program just as it was about to blow out of the stands.

"Maybe the wind will die down before the race starts," Beth said hopefully.

"Maybe." Cindy looked up at the sky. The blowing dust had turned it a pale brown. She doubted if the gale would drop anytime soon.

Programs, food wrappers, and tickets were whirling onto the track. Housewarming, a blue roan just in from the southern tracks, skittered as a piece of paper wrapped around his hoof, then he began to rear in fright. An escort rider dismounted to free the panicking horse. Polish Waltz, the bay Canadian champion, balked as a fierce blast of wind blew dust and grit into his eyes.

I was right about the wind bothering the horses, Cindy thought. *I don't even think they can see very well. I know I can't, and it's worse out there on the dirt. Maybe all Ashleigh's instructions to Felipe won't mean much, since the horses will be fighting the wind.*

Sid Ames, Adieu's jockey, rode close to Felipe. The two jockeys exchanged words.

"What did they say?" Cindy wondered.

"Sid may be trying to psych Felipe out," Ashleigh said. "Sid's known for that around the backside. When I first started riding, he always picked on me whenever he got the chance. You learn to ignore him pretty quickly."

"I don't think he'll have much luck picking on our jockey." Mike laughed. "Felipe grew up in a very tough neighborhood in New York. If anyone gets psyched out, it's going to be Sid."

Just as Glory was loading into the gate, a sudden gust whipped through the stalls, throwing leaves and dust. Glory stopped in his tracks.

"He hasn't balked going into the gate since his maiden race!" Cindy groaned.

"He's not balking—he's just getting his bearings," Ashleigh said. A moment later the gray colt walked into the gate.

Cindy checked the odds board as the rest of the nine-horse field loaded. Adieu was going in as the favorite. Glory was next.

Glory really should be the favorite, Cindy thought with a rush of confidence. *The wind isn't going to stop him from running!*

The starting bell clanged, sounding muffled. The horses broke from the gate and struggled into the gale.

"Glory's in the lead!" Cindy cried. Felipe angled the colt toward the rail just as Adieu's jockey tried to shoot past. But Glory was already ahead of him, up close to the rail in perfect position.

"Attaboy," Ashleigh said with satisfaction.

The rest of the field seemed bewildered by the pressure of the wind blowing them backward. After Glory and Adieu the next horse trailed six lengths back.

"Very slow first quarter as the field heads into the wind," the announcer commented.

So Glory wasn't moving very fast, either. Cindy glanced at Ashleigh. "Is he doing okay?" she asked through gritted teeth.

"For now." Ashleigh didn't take her eyes from the track. "I don't like that slow pace, though. The wind's a factor here—but Glory could pick up the pace if he wanted."

"He's fooling around." Cindy's heart sank as Glory galloped along the backstretch. Glory was in a beautiful position for now, she thought, but the race could still be a repeat of the Jim Dandy.

"I'm not sure what's going on." Ashleigh frowned. Glory's ears were flicking back and forth, as if he were confused.

"Straighten him out, Felipe," Mike muttered. "Don't let him start thinking too much out there."

"Adieu's two lengths back. I wish Felipe would take Glory under a hold and let Adieu catch up— Glory needs another horse to run against," Ashleigh said tersely. "If he doesn't wake up out there, he could be caught by a closer like Adieu. The other horses are settling down, too. The wind's dropping."

"Adieu isn't out of this race at all," Ian said.

"Neither are the others. Here comes the rest of the field!" Ashleigh cried.

Cindy could hardly believe her eyes. With the exception of the number-five horse, who was being eased, the entire field of racehorses was pounding into Glory's lead like a cavalry charge.

Felipe had quickly glanced around and seen them, but Cindy doubted Glory had. With the wind it was probably difficult for the colt to hear the wall of horses coming up behind him. But he could hear Felipe. *Talk to Glory!* Cindy willed the jockey. *Tell him what to do!*

"And the field is mounting a challenge to March to Glory!" the announcer cried. "He's dropping back! But an honest time set for the three-quarter mile."

Cindy felt the blood drain from her face. An honest time! That meant an average pace for an average horse. With Felipe's excellent riding, Glory was running a respectable race. But the colt was capable of so much more, Cindy knew. If only he would give the race his best! He would have to. The other horses had narrowed his lead to a length!

Felipe leaned even farther forward over Glory's neck and seemed to speak to him. At the same instant he turned Glory's head slightly to the outside. Suddenly Glory seemed to see Adieu and the rest of the field at his flank as they rounded the far turn. The big gray colt threw up his head.

What's Glory going to do? Cindy was half out of her seat. *He can't go out of control now!*

Right away she saw that was the furthest thing

from the colt's mind. Glory changed leads and powered clear of Adieu by a length, holding off the other colt's late run as they headed into the stretch. Adieu responded, maintaining his position, but he couldn't close. The rest of the field dropped back.

"And March to Glory has his legs under him," the announcer called. "He's having a perfect trip now!"

The wind kicked up again, blasting the horses with stinging sand. Cindy felt as though a brick had hit her. She pushed her blond hair out of her eyes. When she could see again, she frantically scanned the track.

For a second she thought the wind was pinning Glory's ears so close to his head. Then she realized Glory was angry—angry at the wind for holding him back. The colt found an even higher gear. He was opening up a lead of four lengths on Adieu—then eight, then twelve!

Cindy was barely aware that she was on her feet, screaming. "Faster, Glory! You're flying!" she screeched.

Glory was running so easily now—he was blazing through the fractions! His ears were still swept back against his head as he fought the wind.

Glory looks like Just Victory did when we raced, Cindy thought, dazed. *Glory's running Just Victory's race. Does Glory remember what that was like? Or is now just the first time he's needed that fire?*

"Felipe's hand-riding the colt!" Samantha shouted. "Glory's putting out the effort on his own!"

"He'd circle the field if the race were longer," Mike said in happy disbelief.

"I think he can run through anything!" Cindy was squeezing her hands tightly together.

In the last eighth Glory was beautifully relaxed, drawing off effortlessly. The wind beat against him, but he extended his lead to fifteen lengths. He roared past the finish, a silver streak of motion.

"And it's March to Glory, finishing full of run in the teeth of a headwind of forty miles per hour!" the announcer called. "He's set a track record!"

Cindy flung out her arms in a huge V. "Yes!" she shouted. "Yes, yes!" She and Samantha grabbed hands and did a victory dance.

"That's what I call the right kind of romp," Ashleigh said happily.

"You bet!" Ian agreed.

Standing in the winner's circle, posing for photographs with Ashleigh, Mike, and Ian, was a happy blur for Cindy. Glory was snorting and still excited. He actually laid back his ears when a track dignitary got too close, behavior Cindy associated more with Sierra—or Just Victory.

But Glory was as affectionate as always with Cindy, bumping her and nuzzling her as he asked for attention. He almost knocked her down with his enthusiasm when he urgently checked her pockets for carrots. Cindy quickly led Glory away from the crowd to cool him out, leaving Ashleigh, Mike, and Ian proudly answering the reporters' many questions about Whitebrook's future champion.

Gradually the voices faded. The backside seemed very still to Cindy after the confusion at the track, with the quiet broken only by soft voices and an occasional snort as grooms or trainers led horses to or from the shed rows. Cindy noticed that the wind had died down. Only the sheen on Glory's coat, glittering like silver dust in the sun, remained as a testament to his effort.

Thrilling as all the attention had been, Cindy was glad to get away from it. Nothing could top time alone with her beloved horse.

"You were so wonderful, Glory," Cindy said softly. "Do you know that?"

Glory gave his head a quick toss, as if to say, *Never a doubt.*

"Hi, Cindy!" Anne called. She fell into step beside them. "That was the most incredible race! I watched the finish from right near the rail."

"Wasn't it great?" Cindy said proudly. She was glad to see the other girl. It seemed as if it had been a long time since they'd disliked each other.

"You are so lucky to have this horse." Anne reached out to touch Glory's smooth shoulder.

"I know." Cindy stroked Glory's shoulder, too. A sudden chill went through her at Anne's words. Cindy remembered that she didn't really have Glory—not the way she had before. Now the Townsends owned half of him.

"What's the matter? You just turned awfully pale." Anne looked at her curiously.

"Nothing." Cindy didn't want to talk about the arrangement with the Townsends. She tried to tell herself that maybe it wouldn't be so bad. Mr.

Townsend had promised that Glory would still be well cared for, and he'd still live at Whitebrook. Nothing would change.

"We're going home in a couple of days," Anne said. "My father's not sure what his schedule will be like for the rest of the fall, but he might be at Belmont near Breeders' Cup day." She grinned. "I know you will be!"

"It looks that way." Cindy smiled back, her spirits soaring again. She couldn't wait for the Breeders' Cup—on that day, she was sure, her horse would run to his greatest triumph. "I hope I see you there," she added.

"If we can't get together then, you should come see me at Del Mar sometime," Anne invited. "It's an old track like Saratoga, and just as beautiful. Even if Whitebrook horses aren't racing at Del Mar, you could come up the next time you're at the Santa Anita or Hollywood Park track."

"Thanks—I'd love to see the ocean!" Cindy was thrilled. She knew that her dad usually raced their horses in Florida over the winter, but the previous March he had shipped Shining to Los Angeles for the Santa Anita Handicap, which she'd won. The chances were good that Whitebrook would be running at least one horse at one of the big California tracks that winter or spring—maybe Glory or Shining. Cindy smiled in happy anticipation.

"My family's house is right on the beach," Anne added. "We could go swim in the surf every day and ride the horses next to the ocean."

"Cool!" Cindy tried to imagine what that would be like. Kentucky was landlocked. She'd meant to go to one of the New York beaches with Samantha and Tor, but with the press of taking care of the horses, they hadn't gotten around to it. "I've never been to the beach," she said cautiously. She hoped Anne wouldn't laugh.

"Well, I've never seen a famous horse farm like Whitebrook." Anne smiled. "Maybe someday you'll show me around."

"It's a deal! You're definitely invited." Cindy smiled back.

"See you later." Anne gave Glory a final pat and waved. "I've got to meet my parents."

"Okay." Cindy waved back. *Anne's so nice. You can't always tell what people are like right away*, she thought, then turned to Glory. The colt was walking obediently behind her, occasionally stretching his neck to nuzzle her pockets or hand. "Now it's just you and me, boy," she murmured.

Glory bumped her affectionately with his nose. Even after a stupendous effort such as the one he had just put in, he was as gentle and sweet as ever. Cindy loved the trust her horse had in her.

She walked the colt for another half hour, enjoying the soft, familiar clopping of his hooves on the dirt. Then she crosstied him in the barn for a warm bath.

Glory leaned his head under the hose, obviously relishing the stream of water coursing over his dusty coat. Cindy carefully scraped off the excess water and began toweling him dry.

Glory shook himself hard, splattering water on the walls, grooming implements, and Cindy.

"Gee, thanks, Glory," she said, grinning. "That saves me a lot of work with the towel. Or maybe you're saying I need a bath, too."

When the colt was dry, Cindy combed his mane and tail until they ran like silk through her fingers. Then she stepped back to admire her work.

"You couldn't be more beautiful or more perfect," she said. "This really is your glory day."

Just get it over with, Cindy coached herself the next morning as she walked to the barn. Leaving Glory was one of the hardest things she'd ever had to do. She wanted to say good-bye and leave the colt before she broke down in tears.

After the race the day before, the group from Whitebrook had met Cindy at Glory's stall. After a lot of fussing over the colt, they'd all gone to a steak house and treated themselves to a delicious dinner of thick, juicy filet mignon, scalloped potatoes, and choices from a tray loaded with mousse cake, key lime pie, and other sumptuous desserts. For hours everyone had talked over Glory's brilliant race and his prospects. Mike was already speculating about the colt's four-year-old season the next spring, beginning with a possible run in the Donn Handicap in Florida. In the excitement Cindy had forgotten her worries about Glory and the Townsends.

But now, in the blinding early morning light, Cindy had to face the present. She would be separated from her horse, and now that the Townsends owned half of him, he might be in danger again. That was making her miserable.

Cindy looked over the stall door at Glory. A lump formed in her throat. The colt was contentedly munching the last of his breakfast of grain and hay. In the filtered light of the barn, his dappled coat glowed with health and good conditioning.

Glory looked up from his hay net. With a low whicker he stepped quickly to the door, expecting his usual attention.

Cindy didn't dare move. She was afraid that if she did, the calm she was trying so hard to maintain would shatter. She could easily imagine starting to cry and being unable to stop.

Glory nudged her almost questioningly, as if to say, *What's wrong?*

"Oh, Glory." Cindy closed her eyes against the tears. For one last moment she buried her face in Glory's thick mane and ran her hands over his warm, glossy coat. The memory would have to last her for weeks.

She knew it was time to go. Cindy stepped out of Glory's stall and closed the door. "Good-bye, Glory," she said quietly. "I love you so much."

Glory whickered softly again, as if to say he would miss her.

Cindy turned to leave the barn. She knew her family was waiting in the parking lot, but she couldn't make herself go. What would it be like back home without Glory? Cindy hated to leave the colt even for a school day. This would be much harder.

"I don't care if I miss school," Cindy said defiantly. "I'd rather stay here with you."

Glory cocked his head, listening.

"But they'd just come get me if I did." Cindy sighed heavily. "I guess this isn't good-bye forever—I'll see you in September, or maybe October. It depends on when your next race is." Mike and Ian tentatively planned to run the colt in the Woodward in September or the Jockey Club Gold Cup in early October. Both races were at the Belmont track.

Glory pushed his chest hard against the stall door. *He wants to come with me*, Cindy thought, her heart aching. *I wish he could come instead of Storm's Ransom, even though I like him.* The new colt would be returning to Whitebrook in the trailer and would begin his yearling training soon. Working with Storm was one positive thing about returning home.

"I know I can't take you away, even if Dad would let me," Cindy said to Glory, trying to smile. "You belong here. You're a real racehorse now—you're going to set a track record in every race you run from now on."

Glory tossed his head and snorted impatiently. He seemed to be saying, *Just let me out there.*

"Don't worry, I won't miss the Breeders' Cup," Cindy said, smoothing Glory's long forelock out of his eyes. "You'll be there, you know."

Glory leaned his head into her caresses, begging for more. Cindy laughed and rubbed his ears just the way he liked. *So what if I'm a little late meeting everybody?* she thought. *They know where I am.*

Suddenly Glory spooked, jerking his head out of her arms and backing away from the door. Cindy turned to see what had startled him.

Brad Townsend was standing next to her, slapping his boot with a riding crop.

"What are you doing here . . . Cindy?" he asked irritably.

"I'm Glory's groom," Cindy said, struggling to be polite. "And his exercise rider at home," she added. She couldn't believe that after all she'd done for Glory, Brad seemed barely able to remember her name. Just the tone of his voice set her teeth on edge.

Brad frowned. "Bring the colt out of the stall. I want to take a look at him."

Cindy knew she had to do it—Brad was Glory's co-owner now. Her throat tightening with anxiety, she led Glory out of the stall and clipped a lead line to his halter.

Brad studied Glory and raised an eyebrow. Cindy could see that he was impressed by the colt's superb good looks. She almost wished Glory didn't look so good, because now Brad would be more interested in him than ever.

"Bring him closer." Before Cindy could move, Brad yanked the lead line out of her hand and gave it a sharp pull. Glory threw up his head in warning and stayed where he was. He seemed to be saying, *I can be polite to strangers, but I'm not going anywhere with you.*

"Easy, Glory," Cindy said softly. For his sake she had to try to help him please Brad. Brad just acted worse when he didn't get his way.

Brad walked around Glory. Then he stopped and ran his hands down one of Glory's long, slender legs. Glory stood quietly, but his ears were pricked. He was clearly wary of this stranger and on his guard.

"All right, put him back in the stall," Brad said dismissively. "Sometimes I can't believe how sloppily this horse has been handled. It's no wonder he's acted up. Well, that's going to change now."

Cindy felt her stomach give a sickening lurch. *I knew it!* she thought. *Ashleigh said the Townsends wouldn't interfere with Glory, but they're starting already. And Ashleigh's probably gone back to Whitebrook for good—she can't stop them.*

Silently Cindy led Glory back to his stall. Her heart was pounding, and her hands were slippery with sweat. She couldn't think what to say to Brad. There was never anything to say to Brad, she realized, because he always got his way—no matter what the consequences. Cindy remembered again how the racing careers of Wonder, Pride, and Princess had suffered once the Townsends got involved in their training. Princess had barely survived.

Cindy could visualize so many horror scenes once the Townsends began meddling in Glory's training. What if they tried to overrace him, or Brad had the colt ridden too hard in works, the way he did with his own horses? Ashleigh had said that wasn't going to happen, but in the past she hadn't been able to protect the horses she and the Townsends co-owned. Cindy imagined Brad and Lavinia constantly at Whitebrook, putting their two cents in where they weren't wanted and disrupting Whitebrook's peaceful training center.

Cindy felt a terrible chill crawl down her spine. Only two things were certain about Glory's future now: She had to leave him to go back to school, and the Townsends owned half of him, with major races, including the Breeders' Cup, coming up.

The colt put his head over the stall door, watching her with his usual gentle, curious expression. "You don't understand, do you?" Cindy whispered. Glory didn't know that his whole way of life was threatened.

Cindy hugged Glory's satiny gray neck hard, wishing she could stay there and protect him every minute of the day. But she couldn't.

What will happen to Glory now? Cindy wondered desperately. *Who can stop the Townsends from ruining him?*

Joanna Campbell was born and raised in Norwalk, Connecticut, with her three younger brothers. When she was a child, she owned her own horse, Moe, a chestnut part Quarter Horse. In her early twenties, she took open jumping lessons and competed in cross-country point-to-points. Still an avid horse fan, she recently saw the Breeders' Cup races in Belmont Park, New York. She is the author of twenty-six young adult novels, and four adult novels. She now lives in Camden, Maine, with her husband, Ian Bruce, their dog, Preppie, and their cat, Kiki. She has two children, Kimberly and Kenneth, and three grandchildren, Taylor, Kyle, and Becca.

Karen Bentley was born in Missouri and has lived in Arkansas, Pennsylvania, and New York. As a child, she took English equitation and jumping classes, and as a teenager, she barrel raced. She has bred and raised Quarter Horses, including a horse named Chestnut Kid Alice, which she rode in New York City's Central Park. Karen now lives in Albuquerque, New Mexico, where she rides Chestnut's daughter, Ramey Bar Dazzle, along the Rio Grande. Karen has a six-year-old son named David. She is the author of eight novels for young adults.

THOROUGHBRED

created by Joanna Campbell

Read all the books in the Thoroughbred series and experience the thrill of riding and racing, along with Ashleigh Griffen, Samantha McLean, Cindy Blake, and their beloved horses.